Dear Reader,

What could be mor  *ure
the bride in an exq* *ng
from the glorious* *he
handsome groom in* *es
sparkling with happ* *se
"to have and to hold* *over. . . . This is
the perfect ending to a courtship, the blessed ritual we
cherish in our hearts. And now, in honor of the tradi-
tion of June brides, we present a month's line-up of
six LOVESWEPTs with beautiful brides and gorgeous
grooms on the covers.*

**Don't miss any of our brides and grooms this
month:**

#552 HER VERY OWN BUTLER
     by Helen Mittermeyer
#553 ALL THE WAY by Gail Douglas
#554 WHERE THERE'S A WILL . . .
     by Victoria Leigh
#555 DESERT ROSE by Laura Taylor
#556 RASCAL by Charlotte Hughes
#557 ONLY YOU by Bonnie Pega

*There's no better way to celebrate the joy of weddings
than with all six LOVESWEPTs, each one a fabulous
love story written by only the best in the genre!*

With best wishes,

Nita Taublib

Nita Taublib
Associate Publisher/LOVESWEPT

WHAT ARE *LOVESWEPT* ROMANCES?

They are stories of true romance and touching emotion. We believe those two very important ingredients are constants in our highly sensual and very believable stories in the *LOVESWEPT* line. Our goal is to give you, the reader, stories of consistently high quality that may sometimes make you laugh, sometimes make you cry, but are always fresh and creative and contain many delightful surprises within their pages.

Most romance fans read an enormous number of books. Those they truly love, they keep. Others may be traded with friends and soon forgotten. We hope that each *LOVESWEPT* romance will be a treasure—a "keeper." We will always try to publish

LOVE STORIES YOU'LL NEVER FORGET
BY AUTHORS YOU'LL ALWAYS REMEMBER

The Editors

Loveswept®552

Helen Mittermeyer
Her Very Own Butler

BANTAM BOOKS
NEW YORK · TORONTO · LONDON · SYDNEY · AUCKLAND

HER VERY OWN BUTLER

A Bantam Book / July 1992

Prologue

"I don't like this," Rex Dakeland said firmly. His large hand clamped the phone receiver tightly. He wanted to help his old family friend through his suffering, but not this way. He tried one more time to dissuade Justin. "Look, Mary Justine obviously—"

"Mary Justine was my only child! Now she's gone!" The elderly man's voice crackled with pain and anger. "I have to find out about my grandchildren. That . . . that woman is hiding them, trying to keep them from me."

"Wait a minute, Justin. She *did* inform you about the deaths of your daughter and son-in-law, and they *had* named her the children's guardian in their wills."

"I know, I know, but then she left Chicago, and I've had a hell of a time tracking her down. And, dammit, now I learn she's adopted them!"

"It was her right," Rex said quietly.

"Mary Justine and David have been dead nearly two years. I hadn't even seen them in the year before. . . . The pain of this loss will never be assuaged, Rex. But if I could see my daughter's children, it might mitigate some of the agony." He sighed heavily. "You're the son of my best friend, and the only person I would trust to do this."

"All right. I said I'd go, and I will." Rex grimaced. "I have my references all set, so I should be able to get some kind of job in the town where she's living. Don't worry. I'll ferret out information for you, but God only knows if it's going to bring you peace of mind."

"Thank you, Rex. I know how much I'm asking of you. I can't think of any role more alien to you than spy."

"You can say that again, old friend. You can say that again."

One

The house had been a proud and haughty Victorian grande dame—once.

Perhaps the women who first had graced her high-ceilinged rooms had worn bustles, the gentlemen high, starched collars. They would have been genteel and courteous people. The house would have demanded it.

Now the house merely demanded attention. The grand old lady not only showed her age, but also displayed a distressing lack of personal hygiene. A face-lift wouldn't suffice. She needed an entire body-lift, from basement to roof. The structure listed, damaged by years of unrepaired assaults. Its shingled facade appeared to have been stained brown at one time, the trim done in a rich cream-colored paint. Now those shingles were splintered and dark gray, and the trim's paint was peeling over rotting wood.

The cupola, its one narrow window boarded up, looked like a sad Cyclops.

Rex scowled at the shabby, battered old beauty. His construction company restored buildings like this one. Money—lots of it—an architect, talented workers, were desperately needed here. He shrugged. He loved old houses, but he couldn't let himself get personally involved in the fate of this one. He had to get inside, find out what was going on, then leave. That's what he had promised to do, and he would do it, but nothing more.

He left his rented car, climbed the rutted brown knoll on which the house stood, then strode up the crumbling cement steps to the front door. Noise poured through the open windows on the wraparound porch. There was chaos going on in the house. Ridiculous. Couldn't be. He was looking for a woman with two children, not the Old Lady Who Lived in a Shoe. He pressed the doorbell. It was rusty and emitted an abrasive sound. Needed to be replaced like everything else he'd seen here.

At the growing clamor of childish voices he turned, intending to go back to his car to recheck the address, when the door opened. He turned back and his jaw dropped. "Mickey Mouse?"

A woman glared at him through the eye slits of the mask she wore. "Minnie Mouse. See?" She pointed to the bow on her head before sweeping her hand down the front of her red-and-white polka-dot blouse and miniskirt.

"Oh. How do you do. I'm looking—"

"Get in here. You're late."

"I am?" Rex eyed the life-size cartoon. The voice was feminine, sultry, a wild contrast to the silly, grinning false face. "Ah, there must be a mistake. I'm looking for Andrew Laughlin—"

"LAW-flynn, not LAWK-lyn. Scottish pronunciation, I'm told. Anyway, you're looking at her."

Rex stared at Minnie Mouse long and hard. He'd assumed a woman with a man's first name would be eccentric. He hadn't expected sexy. "Andrew Laughlin?"

Another crashing sound was followed by screams. Pandemonium seemed to reign in the house.

Minnie Mouse looked over her shoulder, then back at him, wincing at yet one more loud bang. "Yes, I am Andrew Laughlin. Look, we don't have time to talk." She sighed. "All right. Here's how it goes. I haven't had a sex change. My father wanted a boy to name after his father. He got me, and he stuck me with the moniker. Though I've shortened it to Drew." She waved her hand, gloved like Minnie's, and the thick fabric fingers spread wide. "Can we please skip any other amenities? I have fifteen kids in there waiting for balloons, so let's get to it. I wouldn't even have called you, if I could have managed the tank of helium myself. Stupid thing's got its valve stuck." She turned and started down the hall, her words floating back to him. "Actually, I'm relieved you're here so quickly. You said on the phone there might be a problem and you might not make it."

"Wait a minute. I'm not the balloon man. . . ." Rex's voice trailed off. He was talking to thin air. Minnie Mouse, or rather Andrew Laughlin, had raced back to the party. She was quite a woman. What the hell? If she needed a balloon man, he'd be one. He'd told himself he'd do anything necessary to get into this house and fulfill his promise to Justin.

He'd seen her ad for "a houseman, general factotum, or butler, whatever," in the local *Penny Saver* free newspaper when he'd been checking out the area a few days back. It was the damnedest ad he'd ever come across, but he'd jumped at it. A job—any job—in her house was just what he needed.

Minnie Mouse's head poked out of a doorway at the end of the long center hall that bisected the house. "Will you get back here? An insurrection of five-year-olds is brewing." Shaking her head, Minnie disappeared.

Rex paused, a slow smile spreading over his face. He was invited to the party. Why shouldn't he go? He strolled down the hall, papered with pink cabbage roses. The wallpaper was in relatively good shape, but there were marks here and there, damp spots and pale spirals of rust. The flooring was random-width oak with a decided list. It needed to be jacked up. Years of taking care of the old house on his farm before going into the construction and restoration business had taught him plenty about sagging structures. But he knew nothing about being a "general factotum, butler, whatever."

So? Could it be that difficult? He kept house for himself pretty much, with a housekeeper coming in every two weeks. He could cook pancakes and scrambled eggs, broil a steak, and do a mean stir fry. Be the balloon man, ingratiate himself, get the job. Best way inside. But, why did she want a butler? Wasn't that for English drawing rooms? He smiled. Didn't matter. He could handle it.

Halfway down the hall he saw it. At first he thought it was a mirage, then a stuffed animal. Then it moved—no, slithered—toward him. "Hey!" Surprise held him in place as the gaudy green creature with the vivid blue forehead eyed him unblinkingly. Left over from the dinosaur age? Man-eater? Rex took a step back. Big. Over three feet long, and maybe eight inches wide at its middle.

Minnie Mouse appeared again. "What's keeping you? Oh. That's just Alonzo. He's an iguana. Tame. He won't hurt you. He's into lettuce." She paused. "Not that he should eat that too much.

Doesn't have the nutrients he needs. He's better with beaten egg or dried mynah-bird pellets."

"Glad to hear it," Rex muttered, not moving, keeping his eyes on the iguana, which was also still.

"Do come on. Just walk around him."

Rex took a deep breath and did so, finding the unblinking stare of the lizard unnerving. "Good boy . . . I think." He got past it! When he heard the *whuff*, he glanced at Alonzo, then looked behind him. A mammoth fuzzy dog eyed him. "Your dog is cross-eyed, Minnie."

"That's Faulkner. And he won't bite unless you're aggressive around the children. He's our watchdog. Mixed big breeds—Saint Bernard, Great Pyrenees, and bloodhound, so the vet says. We found him on our doorstep one day, full of fleas and ticks. He'd scratched himself raw in some places. We had him dipped." Minnie paused to take a breath. "Iguanas are afraid of dogs, usually. Alonzo doesn't fear Faulkner one bit. We can't figure it out. Can we get to the balloons now?"

"Sure." Glancing behind him at the weird twosome, he shook his head and followed Minnie Mouse into total chaos. This was a bona fide nuthouse. Andrew Laughlin was running a loony bin.

Fifteen kids, all in costume, were shouting, punching each other, laughing or chattering. Bits of chips, popcorn, pretzels, littered the hardwood floor that had a decided slant, similar to the one in the hallway.

Minnie Mouse didn't need a butler, she needed a carpenter. The house was falling down.

She shoved a metal tank and a bag of balloons at him, and bellowed for order. "Now, hear this, guys. We're going to have a balloon game. Jamie, don't spit the health mix, please. Cassie, don't cry, you can have a blue balloon. Okay, everybody. Let's go, let's go."

Rex got going! The valve of the helium tank wasn't too difficult to open.

The object of the game must've been to see who could punch his neighbor the hardest, he decided, but after a time, they really got into the balloon game. And the prizes that Minnie gleefully gave out. He pumped up balloon after balloon. When he thought he was all set, that everyone had at least one, there'd be a pop or two, and it would be time to blow up some more.

When he finally was ahead by a few balloons, he chanced a look at his watch. An hour since his arrival! The kids were devouring ice cream and cake now, and he was more partied out than any of the guests. He leaned on the helium tank and took a time-out.

"I'll have another balloon. Ooops. Gee, mister, I'm sorry I got ice cream on you. Your costume looks pretty nice." A gap-toothed boy grinned up at Rex. "Wanna use my napkin?"

"Ah, no thanks. I'll get it later." Send it to the cleaners. Chocolate ice cream and chocolate sauce. Did it come off cotton slacks? Should've worn jeans. No, a Sherman tank would be the best costume. But he'd had to look fairly well dressed. He was applying for a job . . . as a butler.

"That's okay, mister. I made the mess, I'll clean it for you." He smeared the ice cream into a bigger circle. "Gee, this isn't working."

"Nope." Rex smiled. "We'll let the cleaners take care of it."

"Good idea," the boy said.

Kids weren't unknown to Rex. He had an assortment of nieces and nephews. Some lived in California, others near his farm and center of business in the Green Bay area of Wisconsin. He saw all of them on holidays, and the ones in his vicinity more often. He generally enjoyed them—but then he'd never been in the midst of one of their parties.

He ignored his sticky pant leg and blew up more balloons. Again he rested, looked around the hexagon-shaped room. Its leaded-pane windows were beautiful.

He gave the last of the balloons away, then tightened down the tank. The guests were leaving. He followed Minnie down the hall.

"'Bye, Rex. Thanks for the balloons. 'Bye, Alonzo. 'Bye, Faulkner." Voice after voice called out thanks and farewells.

When the door closed, one boy dressed as a pirate and a tiny girl who must've been Glinda the good witch were left.

The boy walked up to Rex. "I know you're Rex. Jimmy Carmichael asked your name, is how I know. Hi, I'm Ira Hampton Laughlin. This is my sister, Louise."

Rex acknowledged the introduction with a big grin.

Minnie Mouse stifled a yawn, taking off her mask and inhaling tiredly. "He is a good balloon man," she said to Ira, then turned to Rex. "How much do I owe you?" She eyed the chocolate-ice-cream-and-sauce smear. "I'll pay for your cleaning."

Rex stared. A knockout. Eyes like aquamarines, slanting upward slightly at the outer corners. Skin like new cream, dimples bracketing her mouth. High, wide cheekbones. He already knew she had great legs. "Ah. What? Yes. I tried to tell you when I first arrived, Miss—"

"Ms, if you don't mind."

Rex swallowed a grin when she eyed him so seriously. "Ms. Laughlin, I'm not the balloon man. I saw your ad for a butler. I'm here to apply for the position." Even with her mouth hanging open and her eyes popping, she was gorgeous. "I don't suppose they get too many ads for butlers in the local paper." He eyed her expectantly as she looked him up and down, then carefully moved in front of the children, glancing sideways at the panting dog. What the hell did she think he was? An ax-murderer?

"What? The paper? Ah, how do I know that? You say you're not the balloon man, but you've been blowing them up for an hour or more." Words ran together in her mind as she touched each child, then relaxed when he made no move toward them. "References," she said, her eyes snapping.

"I have them with me, in the car. I'll get them." He went around her and out the front door on the run. He didn't want her to change her mind about the job or regret the ad. He made it to the car and back into the house in record time. "Here they are."

She leaned back against the wall wainscoted in dark, pitted mahogany, looking tired . . . and sexy. She expelled air upward, setting aflutter the damp, curling hair on her forehead. "Ad, did you say?" At his nod she groaned. "That's been running for weeks. In the *Clarion* too. I forgot to withdraw it." She shrugged. "I thought a houseman would be nice. . . ." Her voice trailed. "I don't think we could afford you now. I'd better call today and get the ad pulled." She moved her shoulders expressively. "I thought *The New York Times* was going to buy my article on sexual harassment. They didn't. I'm a free-lance writer. I've been in the Ithaca papers and the ones in Binghamton and the

Chronicle in Rochester. Once in the *Star* in Syracuse." She shrugged. "But *The New York Times* . . . That would've put us over, financially. They showed a great deal of interest initially, then turned down the piece. But why am I telling you all this?" Her shoulders slumped. "Hot for early June."

"Yes," Rex said. He took a deep breath. "Ms. Laughlin, my name is Rex Dakeland, and I'd like the job as your butler. The situation on the lake suits me, and I'm pretty handy. And I don't expect a great deal of money." He named a ridiculously low figure. "Plus room and board. How does that sound? Then, maybe when your financial situation is on the upswing, you could give me a raise."

Drew stared at him, only the grandfather clock in the foyer making a sound. She glanced at the references. "I'll call about these. And I want to see identification—driver's license, even your birth certificate if you have it." Looking down at the papers in her hand, she nodded. "And the last two places of employment." She looked up. "And a rundown on your family, please. Any problems?"

"Nope."

"Too good to be true. You're not a serial killer, are you?" She smiled weakly. She could afford him at the figure he'd mentioned.

He pointed at the references. "You could call some of these right now." He'd made sure his lawyer would have people monitoring any calls from Andrew Laughlin.

"I wike him," Louise lisped, grinning. "And I'm free."

"She means she likes you and she's three," Ira translated patiently.

Louise looked indignant.

"I understood you, Louise."

Louise beamed at him.

"She must like you. She likes to talk to people, but she doesn't tell them she likes them unless they're special," Ira explained, smiling at his sister when she pouted.

Rex held his breath when Drew looked down at the little girl, then back at him. He held his smile in place with great effort. He wanted to tell her he was there under false pretenses and give her the truth. He didn't want to start off on the wrong foot. But he'd say nothing. He'd promised.

"How about a trial? Three weeks? And I can get more references, if you wish." Rex saw her indecision and moved in for the kill. "And you needn't pay me for those three weeks if I'm not suitable. Just room and board."

"Do it, Mommy," Ira urged. "Alonzo likes him, so does Faulkner."

"I wike him," Louise added decisively.

Minnie Mouse was cautious. Rex gauged her carefully. And she didn't quite trust him. He hated the deception. But, dammit, there wasn't any other way.

Drew pushed herself from the wall. "All right, we have a short-term deal. Three weeks from today. And I may want those other references. Now it's cleanup time, birthday boy. You, too, Louise."

"Might as well get started. I'll help," Rex said, pushing his advantage.

Drew looked disconcerted for a moment. "In those clothes? Dress cottons. Pretty nice dress for a balloon man." She closed her eyes as though in pain. "I know, I know. You weren't the balloon man. You were applying for a job." She focused on him again. "Well, you shouldn't clean up with those duds on, even with the stain. You'll find some coveralls in the summer kitchen, big closet along one side. They're worn and paint-spattered, but clean." She pointed in the direction of the kitchen.

"Great," Rex called as he went back down the center hall.

"And bring your clothes to me. I'll send them to the cleaners." She raised her voice because he was almost to the kitchen. He seemed to pause reluctantly, turning to her with a smile.

"No need to bother. I'll have to wear them when I go back to Ithaca to get the rest of my things. I'll take care of it." He disappeared into the kitchen.

Drew stared after him. "Ummm." She had her

houseman, even if he didn't look like one or dress the part. She'd watch him . . . carefully. And she'd check him out very thoroughly.

"Don't worry. He's nice. I know. He fixes b'loons," Ira said helpfully.

"Yes, he does," Louise concurred.

"Let's go, Louise. I'll show you my presents again."

" 'kay."

"Do your picking up first," Drew said absently. She watched them go, her brow creased. "He fixes b'loons. What an endorsement," she muttered. And he was so damned good-looking. Too damned good-looking for a butler . . . and for her own comfort.

Oh, Lord, she hoped she wouldn't regret her decision to let him stay. Her instincts told her he was a good man, but since taking on the responsibility of mothering her best friend's children, she'd had to go beyond instincts. She couldn't shrug things off any longer; she couldn't take any chances that might put the children in jeopardy. Of course, she had known when she placed the ad that she would be taking a risk employing a strange man. But, she had told herself then and reminded herself now, it was a small risk when one thoroughly checked references. And she was going to do that first thing tomorrow. This man-about-the-house she was hiring was much needed. He would vastly improve everyday life for her and the children.

The children. How she loved them. She would never get over the loss of Mary Justine, her dearest pal. But now she loved Mary Justine's two little ones with all her might, as fiercely as if they'd been born under her heart, not in it.

She shook herself out of her reverie and cupped her hands around her mouth. "Enough with the presents. Cleanup time, remember? Take a room." Knowing the worst room would be the kitchen, she headed there, smothering a moan. She hated housework; she was a rotten cook. Being in a kitchen was enough to give her indigestion. She also knew that if the kitchen wasn't tackled first, it would be too painful to look at last.

When she entered the huge room with its twelve-foot ceilings, she stopped dead. Rex was up to his elbows in soapsuds. "We have a dishwasher. Burpy, temperamental, loud, but it does the job," she said faintly.

Rex looked over his shoulder, noting how long and shapely her legs were in the red stockings, how the ruffly polka-dotted miniskirt showed them to advantage. "I'll take care of this. You can help the kids."

"I can?" She both appreciated and resented his efficiency. After all, it was her house. And if she wanted to start in the hated kitchen, wasn't it her choice? She looked at the mountain of casserole dishes and broiler pans from the outdoor cooker and sighed. "I'll start in the living room and the porch."

"Mommy, Louise and me are doing the dining room."

"Be careful. Nothing too heavy." She paused at the large dining room.

"Oookay," Louise said, scooping paper cups into a plastic bag. "I clean."

"Don't forget. Plastics in blue box. Paper in red box. Glass I will do. Metal in green box. What's the magic word?"

"Byy-cycles," Louise shouted.

"Ree-cycle," Ira corrected.

Rex, elbow-deep in soapsuds, listened to the interchange in the kitchen. He came from a wild and woolly family where everyone helped out, all were assigned chores, and mischievous behavior was punished by the transgressor being assigned to do the neighbors' chores or to help out in the local hospital. God, hard work, family, country, his grandfather often said, were the only words that matter. They'd been a rollicking bunch, happy most of the time.

That's what Drew Laughlin had with her two. And all three were damned attractive. The children had light blue eyes that contrasted wonderfully with their beautiful blue-black hair. Drew had reddish-blond hair and eyes the color of the Caribbean Sea on a sunshiny day.

But whereas the children's creamy skin would tan easily, her white, white skin would not. Of course there would be a difference, they weren't her biological children.

But they were a family, an apparently happy family. They loved each other. It bothered him that he could badly disrupt that. Stop, he told himself. What he was doing was right. He'd promised. And that's all he had to remember. It wouldn't make it any easier. But he'd said he'd do it, and he would. It was still a shock that Andrew Laughlin, pronounced Law-flyn, was such a stunning woman.

Drew saw how preoccupied her new house-man was. Watching him from the hall door-way, she had to wonder what he was thinking. When Alonzo moved slowly by her toward the sink and his dish of meal, she was about to warn Rex, then thought better of it. She saw how he caught the movement of the iguana from the corner of his eyes as he set a dish on the drainer.

His hand froze. The creature's unblinking stare unnerved him. But he laughed. "You intimidate me, Alonzo. Are you supposed to?"

"He won't hurt you," Drew whispered, smiling when Rex looked over his shoulder at her. "We didn't know he'd grow this large. You see, we found him by the highway. At first we thought he was dead. Then he moved. We brought him home and called Cornell University to have him checked. We put ads in the paper, but no one claimed him, so we've come to believe he was abandoned where we found him."

"Do you take in all strays?"

Drew hesitated, then smiled. "Even butlers."

Rex sucked in his breath. She was a beauty, and, unconsciously, sexy as hell. Those tiny dimples on either side of her mouth didn't seem real. And her smile would've brought down the walls of Jericho, soundlessly. "I should be finished in here in a few minutes," he managed to say. "When I'm done, I'll go back into Ithaca for the rest of my things, if that's all right." When her smile widened, the dimples deepening, his heart thudded out of rhythm, desire stirring deeply. "Maybe I could take the children swimming tomorrow. It's supposed to be very hot. You, too, of course."

"Don't worry, I'll be there. I've gotten in the habit of being in the water when the children are. I feel safer that way. I assume you can swim."

"Yes." He'd been on the swimming team at the University of Wisconsin, as well as on the baseball team.

"Good. I should warn you, the water here is very cold. Though we've had a warm May and June, Cayuga Lake is deep, especially where we are, and it's spring-fed. So, it never gets really warm."

"I can live with it. I come from Wisconsin." He could've bitten his tongue when her eyes narrowed and she took a wary stance. "Green Bay."

"Ah, the Packers."

She watched him closely. He plunged ahead. "Do you know Wisconsin?"

"I've been to Madison." For Mary Justine and David's wedding. That seemed light-years ago. And she'd never return to Madison, or any other part of Wisconsin. Mary Justine's father lived in that state. He'd been furious at the elopement. Maybe he still was. She pushed herself away from the doorjamb. "I have some straightening up to do upstairs—"

"I can do that."

"No, I'd rather you finished the kitchen. That's the biggest job." Could he know Mary Justine's father? Unlikely. Madison was the capital—large, busy, filled with people. Green Bay? She had to wonder if he'd played for the Packers. He had the height, the massive shoulders, the narrow hips, of a running back. But his face clearly had never been bashed; his nose couldn't ever have been broken. Probably not a pro-football player. She smiled quizzically as she sauntered out of the kitchen.

Rex had seen the myriad questions, the speculation, that raced across Drew's gorgeous face. Sighing, he wished he could begin all over with her. She was beautiful . . . marvelous with the children . . . fun . . . and, he realized with a start, he wanted her. The longer he stayed in her house, the more alienated she was going to be when the truth came out. And it would. Dammit.

Two

Rex had gotten up with the sun. He'd slept well in the cottage at the rear of the house that Drew had assigned to him, and he was raring to go when the children came to the kitchen for breakfast. He'd congratulated himself on having handled that meal well, the cleanup afterward too. He had worked his way through the mopping and dusting of the downstairs rooms with only an occasional curse when he banged an elbow or knee. At just past eleven he was vacuuming, when he felt a tap on his arm.

"We swim now," Ira announced, cocking his head. "Mommy said you'd take us. And she'll come too."

"Good. I'm ready for a break." Rex smiled at the boy. "It won't take more than five minutes for me to get into my trunks. You and your sister play on the beach until I get there. Don't go in the water, understand?"

Ira grinned. "Yep."

As Rex walked down the sloping lawn a few minutes later, he noted how the concrete was disintegrating on the steps leading to the slatted bridge that crossed to the boathouse, which wasn't in much better condition. The whole estate was falling to pieces. He sighed. He could and would do something about all this. In fact, one of the phone calls he'd made from Ithaca the night before when he'd gone there to pick up his things had been about this very matter. Actually, the idea of fixing up this place exhilarated him. There were some lovely features he relished bringing back to their original beauty, for example the hexagon-shaped room in the front of the house with a protruding side bay that had a fabulous view of Cayuga Lake. And he loved the setting here, as well as the countryside beyond. He hadn't known before his search for Andrew Laughlin that New York State had such wide-open spaces. The herds of cattle he'd seen from roads nearby reminded him of his own dairy farm in Wisconsin. His place paid for itself and was managed by three of his cousins, so he had ample time for his construction business and for enjoying the rural area in which he lived.

Perhaps, he thought as he neared the beach where the children played with Drew, he could lessen the impact of his pretense by making improvements on the house and grounds. He shuddered. Drew was going to be furious and feel betrayed when it all hit the fan. He just prayed he'd have enough time to win his way into her good graces before the truth came out.

Now, he vowed, he was going to enjoy this time to play. They had a fine day for the beach. It was hot. The lake was clear as glass, its surface rippling with a light breeze, sailboats dotting the horizon.

"Cold," Louise said as he arrived.

"Need a jacket, little one?"

"Nah," Ira answered Rex. "She likes the water as much as I do. We're gonna go in now."

Drew smiled at her bemused "butler" as the children, squealing with excitement, galloped into the shallows of the lake. "They love the lake. They've been dunking themselves since May. I end up blue and out of breath. Not them."

Rex watched as she removed her terry-cloth robe, her gaze never leaving the children. He caught his breath. He'd expected Drew would have a good figure; he hadn't expected a spectacular one. The nipples of her lovely breasts were strained against the Lycra one-piece suit she wore; her hips were beautifully curved. And her gorgeous legs were even longer than he'd imagined. Andrew Laughlin was a beauty, a real knockout. The white-hot lightning of desire sizzled through him.

Drew turned to Rex, trying not to let the shock she felt register on her face when she saw him in his Riviera briefs. Good heavens, he was Hercules come to life! And, she thought wryly, he surely could have played for the Packers with those muscular long legs, that powerful chest with its arrow of black hair ending tantalizingly in those briefs. His silvery gray eyes and the ebony hair curling around his face completed the picture of a man who was devastatingly handsome and impossibly virile.

Realizing she was gaping, Drew turned her head to look at the children. She swallowed hard. She'd been too busy becoming a parent and establishing herself as a free-lance writer to get involved with a man during the last year plus. Now, though, she was virtually panting for this man she'd just hired. A peculiar hot, fluttering feeling laced her middle, and she wondered if she'd have the strength to keep her fingers from threading through his luscious chest hair.

Throwing down her towel, she did something she'd counseled the children to be wary of—she ran to the water and plunged into the chilly crystal-green depths. Gasping, she surfaced and struck out hard. Then, feeling stretched and more balanced, she surface-dived and turned under water, flashing back the way she'd come.

When she came up against something hard, she surfaced again, sputtering. "Wha—?"

"I thought you were crossing," Rex said, mildly. "Too far without a boat." She wasn't only lovely and sexy as hell, she was quite an athlete as well. "You're quite a woman, boss lady." He didn't realize he'd voiced his thoughts until he saw her pull back and frown. "Sorry. I was being admiring, not denigrating."

Drew relaxed, treading water with him. "All right. I admit that I can be prickly about remarks that could be taken as sexist." Her smile twisted. "I like being a woman. I like who I am, who I can be. I don't tolerate anyone putting that down." He had a great smile . . . and as close as his shave might've been first thing this morning, he already had a tinge of blue on his beard-line.

"What are you thinking, Ms. Laughlin?" He matched her overhand stroke as they headed back to the frolicking children.

"Might as well call me Drew. Everyone around here does. It's an informal community." She grinned, letting the lake water slide into her mouth before expelling it. "To tell the truth, Rex Dakeland, I was thinking that you need to shave twice a day." She laughed out loud when his jaw dropped and he sank into the water. She stroked hard over to the children. "Who wants to go out for a swimming lesson?"

"Me," they chorused.

"All right, Ira, I'll take—"

"I'll take him," Rex said, moving around her, still shaken at how affected he'd been by her remark. "You take Louise, she'll be lighter."

"Wait, Dakeland. Don't go out too far. Neither child can swim. They've begun learning, but they haven't reached any level—"

He reacted soothingly to the rising tenor of her voice. "I've taught swimming at summer camps. I'm careful."

"Good." But she didn't move after picking up Louise. She watched Rex with Ira. When she was satisfied that he was a competent teacher, she swam out with the little girl. "Now, ready?" At Louise's nod and excited grin, Drew slid around so that she was under the child. "Stroke. Thatta girl." Drew loved playing in the water with the children. Though it was cold, the water was refreshing, and the thrashing child above her loved it too.

Rex looked over at Drew. She was totally unconscious of her lethal looks. He wasn't. And she loved the children. This was no put-on emotion. There was a heart-tearing reality about her connection to the boy and girl. He glanced down at Ira, churning with determination in his arms. "Great form. Olympic material."

Ira nodded, swallowing a mouthful of water.

Rex lifted him above the water. "Good boy. Easy does it."

"I'm all right." Ira strained to be free.

The four frolicked in the water, then staggered out on the beach to grab for towels.

"That was fun." Drew chuckled. "You two will need a nap."

"Not yet," Louise said guardedly.

"Not yet," Drew concurred, earning a wide grin.

The children began digging in the sand and stone beach, planning roadways, paths, and walls.

Drew looked over at her new butler. Heavens, the man had a build. Rex laughed at the way she was staring at him. "Sorry. But you don't look like a butler."

"We can't all look like Jeeves."

Weird, Rex thought, he'd begun to really like butlering, if the work he did for Drew and the children could be called that. He was actually a jack-of-all-trades in this house. For the last two weeks he'd been doing general housework, carpentry, plumbing. He even cooked. Most tasks he'd done pretty well, he believed, though he hadn't touched the laundry since the day he'd put two new colored items, a red shirt and blue socks, in with the whites, and the sheets had come out a dismal shade of lavender-gray.

"Not right, huh?" he'd asked Drew as they looked at the dingy linen. "How can I fix it?"

She'd smiled weakly, shaken her head. "Let me do it. I don't mind laundry . . . uh, and I'll handle the silverware and china too."

He'd winced. "You really liked that platter I broke, didn't you? I'm sorry. Take it out of my pay." When she'd laughed, he'd been shaken. By her dimples. Dimples. They were unexpected . . . adorable . . . as outrageously sexy as her legs, her figure, her voice.

And he was impressed with her mothering skills. Drew instinctively seemed to know if something was wrong with either child, and she'd drop everything to try to make it right. That she'd drop everything for them Rex deemed highly significant, because he knew she was in difficult straits financially. She kept to a very strict budget and worked long and hard at her free-lance writing assignments to make ends meet. Yet she rarely lost her temper, although the children, good, healthy specimens that they were, could sometimes test the patience of a saint.

Drew's shouts had brought them all out into the hallway to the foot of the staircase one day last week.

"All right, who brought Alonzo up to my office?" Drew had stormed downstairs carrying the lizard. "He's just nibbled two pages of my article."

Long-faced, Ira had watched as Drew descended the stairs and deposited the lizard on the dry oak floor. He sighed. "How long do I have to sit in the chair?"

"Ten minutes," Drew had announced, pointing to the small chair positioned in the hall near the foyer. "And while you're there, you can clean those crayon marks off the wall. That was your doing, I believe."

"I took Alonzo up," Ira said contritely, "'cause I didn't want you to be lonesome."

"Thank you for the thought, but you know the rule: Alonzo stays on the first floor."

Ira nodded before dashing into the kitchen for paper towels and cleaner. When he took his place on the chair, Louise went to stand beside him and give directions on spraying the marks.

Drew backed toward the kitchen, Rex alongside her. She went straight to the refrigerator for ice water.

"Don't look so sad," Rex told her. "You weren't too hard on Ira."

She smiled wanly. "I'm never sure about discipline. Too much? Not enough?" She shook her head. "I guess I'll always wonder if I'm doing the right thing."

Rex shrugged. "Judgment calls are tough. But you make the children understand without hurting them. And you're consistent . . . that's the most important thing, I think. Keeping to the rules you've set." Drew's beaming smile of relief almost made him stagger. Dear Lord, she was lovely. It wasn't just her great skin and thick hair, her beautiful body. Andrew McLaughlin was as beautiful inside as out. How could he want her so completely when they'd known each other for such a short time—and when he couldn't even let her know who he really was?

Now, as he scrubbed the kitchen floor, his experiences during the past days with Drew and the children, but especially with Drew, burned in his memory. The children had been wild with excitement all day, anticipating a long weekend camping with the families of two neighbors. He'd be alone with Drew. . . . He turned at the sound of footsteps, sloshing soapy water on himself.

Drew chuckled.

"Did you get the kids off?" Although she nodded, he could tell she felt bereft. He stood up and moved close to her. "You're worried about Ira and Louise?"

"No, of course not. I wouldn't have let them go if I were. I'm glad they have the chance to go camping, especially with Rita and Laura, their husbands, and their children."

Rex felt light-headed. Drew smelled of mint, sweet basil, wild oregano. No doubt she'd gone directly to her herb garden after dropping off the children. Sweet, tangy, sexy. That was Drew.

"It's . . . it's just that the children haven't

ever been away from me for an overnight . . ." Drew's whispery voice trailed off. "It's crazy," she added shakily, then turned away and left the kitchen.

Rex watched her go, then listened as she trudged up the stairs. It took all the willpower he possessed to stay where he was. He wanted to go after her, catch her up in his arms, cuddle her, tell her he understood how she felt because he, too, would miss the children and worry a little about them.

The rest of that day Drew confined herself to her office. It was the perfect opportunity for Rex to size up the place and decide where he would want to start renovations. He seized it and began to poke around in the basement. Later he went over the first floor inside and out. Support jacks would come first, of course, and a major check for dry rot. By the time he called it a day, he was dog-tired but happy. He had a long list of what he needed to do the job that had become very, very important to him.

The next day, with the children gone, the house was very quiet. Drew worked. Rex went into town, bought heavy jacks and began adjusting them for the basement. It was going to be a long and tedious job to bring things plumb and level, and there'd be lots of restorative carpentry along the way if his surmise was correct about how extensive the dry rot was.

Late in the day Rex watched Drew through the kitchen window. She had on a pair of scruffy short shorts, a skip hat, a man's shirt with the sleeves rolled, and beat-up sneakers with a rip on the side. She was hoeing the kitchen garden, removing weeds, adding straw between rows and fertilizer to the plants. She looked sexy as hell.

"Damn," he muttered, "why'd I meet her now, this way?"

Flinging off his carpenter's apron, he pushed open the back door and headed for Drew.

As though she sensed him, Drew straightened and turned, her smile hesitant. "Hello, Rex. Is there a problem?"

"No. I've finished my chores, and I was wondering if you'd like to swim, then drive into Ithaca and get a bite to eat?" He could've laughed at the expression of surprise that flashed across her face. But it irritated him too. She couldn't trust him. He shifted his shoulders uncomfortably. Damn. She was wise to question his moves, every one he made. How he hated that.

"Ah . . . swimming. Yes, I'd like that. It's hot out here. But, Ithaca . . . I don't—"

"Why don't you wait and see how you feel after our swim? I'm eager to spend a little of my pay. And I don't know the town well. I know about Cornell, but . . ." He let his voice trail, smiling.

"Ah, Cornell. Yes, named after good old Ezra Cornell."

"I've heard of him," Rex said softly, watching her intently. Blankly, she stared back at him. As though she saw something in his eyes, she blushed. Was his lust showing? She was a vibrant woman, yet restrained and bright as hell. What man wouldn't be intrigued—and turned on by her?

When his smile widened, she frowned and looked away. "I'll get into my suit." Head down, she moved around him.

"See you," he whispered. She must know he wanted her, or at least suspect. He sighed heavily. There was no phone in his cottage, and he couldn't use the one in the main house. He'd have to call Justin from town, talk to him, persuade him to free him from his promise. He had to level with Drew.

He met her just as she stepped outside. "Hi, again." He eyed her terry robe, knowing that the luscious body within its folds was going to drive him mad. His blood pounded as he thought about her removing that robe.

"You're staring."

"Sorry." He forced himself to look out at the lake, but all he saw was Drew . . . Drew . . . Drew.

"Apology accepted," she said lightly.

"I like the boathouse," he muttered.

Drew chuckled. "You don't see too many Italianate boathouses. It's one-of-a-kind around here."

"I'd like to paint it—after I've done work on the main house, of course."

Startled, she shook her head. "No. You can't, Rex. It's too big a project for me to take on right now. I simply don't have the money to do anything to the house—not to paint it, repair it, nothing."

He shrugged. "Why don't I see what kind of deals I can get on some scaffolding and other things? I'll give you a ballpark figure then and—" He broke off as she more vigorously shook her head. "Why not?"

"I had a price quoted to me," she told him. "Too stiff."

"Okay, but what if I can get paint at a very low price, some college kids to do the work, could you manage it?"

"Oh, Rex, think about it. Fifty feet to the top of the cupola. The interior of the house is over three thousand square feet. Figuring the outer dimensions alone, it would take about four acres of paint to cover all that wood. And before painting, the wood has to be scraped. An army is needed for all that work. Not to mention the brushes, rollers, putty and putty knives, the sealers, scrapers. I'll stop the list right there." Drew hauled in a deep breath. "It's out of the question, Rex. I don't see the money in my budget for that kind of work for several years."

"Just let me check it out, Drew. Look into wholesale." Rex was calculating quickly how much he could get by with.

"Don't think I don't appreciate all you want to do . . . what you've started on already." She eyed him soberly. "I'll pay you for those jacks you've purchased. Don't think I haven't seen all you've been up to." Drew bit her lip. She could reimburse Rex from money set aside for the children's clothing. She had a bit to spare there.

"Don't worry about it. The lumber company was tossing them out. All I had to do was haul them here. Didn't cost a cent," he lied glibly. Drew's palpable relief was his reward. How slim was the shoestring she was living on? Too damned slim, apparently. He ached to take all the financial burdens off her shoulders. The damned great barn of a house and the grounds and outbuildings were just too much for Drew to take on.

Smiling to herself, happy she wouldn't have to dip into the clothing money, she shrugged out of her robe.

Rex sucked in his breath. Drew knocked him out. He needed the frigid waters of the lake— and immediately—if he wasn't to embarrass himself.

"Last one in does the weeding tomorrow," he

said, grinning. He dropped his towel and raced for the water.

Drew yelped and raced after him, noting that he was tanned to the line of his briefs. And beyond? Even as the thought crossed her mind, she plunged into the clear green water, gasping from the coldness. The sharp, crisp lake water covered her. It was instantly refreshing, an analgesic to the mind, and she reveled in it. Pushing hard, she forced her body into the depths, not surfacing until her lungs were bursting.

She came out of the water like a wild sea nymph, crystal beads cascading off her; the sun glinting on the droplets made them gold, silver, and diamond jewels on her skin. "Wonderful," she said, then laughed out loud and turned on her back, stroking vigorously.

Rex moved with her. "You're an excellent swimmer, boss lady."

"So are you." And, she thought, he heated up the water with his animal magnetism.

Companionably, they stroked parallel to the beach; then, as though on signal, they made their way back.

Rex felt the usual release of tension that swimming brought, the relaxed vigilance that he'd come to expect from the sport.

When Drew put her feet down and began wading in, he joined her. "What time would you like to drive into Ithaca?"

"Well, that's a long way in and—"

"What about the Taughannock Farms Inn? I've heard that's good, if you don't want to go all the way into the city."

"You know about the inn? Why didn't you apply there for a job?" She stared at him, trying to see beyond his bland smile.

She didn't trust him. Wise woman. Rex gritted his teeth and tried to smile at the reserved, sensuous woman who faced him. "I didn't want to be a waiter or groundskeeper—the only positions available there. I was more intrigued by butlering."

Drew nodded slowly. "We could go to Taughannock this evening, I suppose. I like the food there."

"Great." Relief that she'd made that much of a concession flooded through him. He'd be with her. They'd talk. Maybe for a hour he'd forget why he'd come East, even if he was grateful that however much he hated the reason, he wouldn't have missed meeting Drew Laughlin. "I like the water here," he said slowly. He suppressed a gasp of pleasure when she grinned in answer. Those adorable dimples, those eyes.

"Me too. Actually, I love it. I always have. The swimming is so great. So is the fishing." She hesitated, her smile fleeting. "Though I don't do any."

Rex watched her as she preceded him to the house. He held the screen door as they entered the kitchen. "Why don't you fish?" He inhaled her essence as she passed him. Not perfume, but a personal spicy sweetness that came from her.

"I can't stand seeing the fish choke to death in the air," she said simply.

He stared at her, then shrugged. "I guess I never looked at it that way."

"Fish don't do any better out of water than we do in it without equipment. I expect there'll come a time when I won't eat any fish at all because I'll have dwelt on the way they're killed. Put it down to stupid imagination." Drew left the kitchen by the back staircase.

"Or an excess of caring," Rex murmured to Drew's retreating figure.

Three

Rex walked out onto the small porch of his cottage. He hadn't brought much in the way of dinner clothes, but he had a few good things with him. Subdued. Casual, but a little dressy. Nothing too expensive or stylish. He had decided to wear pearl-gray slacks with a matching shirt, a coral linen sports coat, and gray leather loafers. He just hoped that Drew wouldn't recognize the Gucci design and craftsmanship in his shoes. A small mistake, those loafers. Beyond that, he wondered what she would think about the way he looked. He couldn't remember a time since adolescence when such a question had passed through his head. Ah, what that woman was doing to him.

And what would Drew think of his 1980 Mustang? His car looked beat up, but had the guts of a Porsche inside. He'd replaced the engine himself with the help of friends. And he'd raced it a few times with some success. Shipping it here had been an indulgence, and he'd done it for two reasons. He loved the car, which also wouldn't break down, and he believed that Drew wouldn't think it unusual for a working man to own it. She wouldn't guess there was a premium engine underneath the disreputable-looking hood.

He crossed the lawn, intending to go in the back door, but Drew was coming out, so he waited in the relative shade of the huge pin oak that overhung the house. Wearing a pale yellow dress, she looked like a flower—a buttercup or daffodil. Her tanned legs, curvy and long, looked even sexier in the medium-heeled sandals. Simply dressed as she was, she had an innate style and grace, a confidence in her taste. She was so lovely, Rex could scarcely catch his breath. "What do they call that material?" he asked as he walked out of the shade into the sun to meet her.

Drew spun around. "I didn't hear you."

Again there was a suspicion in her eyes. Damn. "Sorry." She relaxed a bit, but her smile was tentative.

She lifted the skirt of the dress a trifle. "It's called cotton batiste. It's the coolest I have."

"And in ninety five-degree heat it's a good idea." The heat he felt when he looked at her didn't come from the temperature.

"Yes. Who would ever figure we'd have such weather in June? May was about the same. That doesn't usually happen in upstate New York."

"Unprecedented, I imagine," he said absently, knowing very little about the climactic ups and downs of the region but mesmerized by her lemon-yellow beauty. She was a *rara avis*, and wholly unconscious of her unique charm. Maybe that was why she was so sensuous. There was certainly nothing calculating about her.

She couldn't help but stare at him. Understated. But, oh so sexy. He exuded confidence, quiet sophistication. He was too much man with his muscular physique, his twist of a smile, his bedroom eyes. Why didn't he turn her cold? Cold? Laughable. He burned her. Ridiculous. But when he handed her tea or coffee, sometime she could almost feel his masculine power. Yet with the children he was inexpressibly gentle, sweet. The man was an outrageous anomaly. One minute he was so sexy she reeled, the next he was leaning over a cookbook, a ruffled apron tied around his waist, his lips moving as he checked out a recipe. And wasn't he an odd sort of man to have responded to her ad? It didn't make sense that he wanted such a position. She frowned, then asked in a tone that she hoped sounded casual, "You seem to have done a great many jobs, and I wonder which was your favorite."

Rex heard the forced tone in her voice. "I'm a pretty good mechanic, but I guess I like construction best," he told her honestly. "One of the reasons I'd like to work on your house."

"Oh," she murmured. His answer made sense, but she should question him further. She was distracted again, though, by his looks. He bore a marked resemblance to the actor Richard Gere, and he was dressed as though he had a yacht parked in the harbor in front of the club.

Rex smiled at her. "I'm looking forward to this evening. I've done a great deal of my own cooking since my arrival, so it'll be a relief to taste something well prepared." He unwound a bit when the dimples appeared. Then she chuckled. His heart thudded against his breastbone as desire thundered through him. She was an artless Circe. He bowed. "The chariot awaits . . . though it's not quite a chariot."

Drew glanced toward the driveway, then blinked at the "chariot." "Does it run?"

"Very well," Rex answered truthfully. "I just haven't gotten around to fixing the outside."

Drew nodded understandingly. "Money. I know the feeling. I put things off until I've got the money in hand. Otherwise, I'd be in the suds."

"A new paint job would cost money," Rex

hedged. He wanted to tell her that he could afford it, that he could afford to wine and dine her. And that he wanted to do just that for about a thousand nights running.

He'd almost stopped questioning why she commanded all his thoughts. Smile. Shape. Warmth. Compassion. Mind. Sense of humor. Dignity. Good reasons . . . but there was more. Andrew Laughlin had moved into his being. He'd begun to breathe in time with her, his blood pulsing in time with hers.

"I'm in the car. You can close the door now," Drew said gently, wondering what had absorbed him so quickly. Was he married? It was like swallowing a boulder even to think such a thing. And it was stupid to react like that. She had the children and her career; she didn't have time for anything, or anyone, else.

He slipped under the wheel, turning to watch her. "I'm not the only one daydreaming," he said softly.

She reddened. "I was thinking of the children," she said in half-truth.

"You love them."

"They're my life."

Rex felt jolted to his toes. As he started the car, he had to fight down the overwhelming urge to tell her everything.

At the muted roar of the engine Drew turned to him. "Twin cams? What a carburetor! You built this?" Suspicion again flashed across her face.

Surprise at her knowledge of cars had him speechless for a second. "I didn't build it. I did negotiate for the engine. Two people I knew in Wisconsin had foreign-car franchises. I traded services for the motor." That was true enough. It'd been his construction company that had built his best friend's house. As an added inducement, Rob had dangled the carrot of the Porsche engine in front of him. He hadn't been able to resist.

"What services?"

"Construction," Rex answered flatly, deciding then and there that he wouldn't lie to her, and if she pushed him into a corner, he was going to be up-front with her. "I'm a pretty fair handyman."

"Modern-day butler," Drew murmured, smiling.

"Exactly." Settling back, he accelerated, loving the power under him, gearing down into it, the car zooming up the steep road leading from the lake road to the highway. The car roared over the hilly, curving highway that edged Cayuga Lake for its forty and more miles in length.

He felt her hard stare without turning to look at her. "What?"

"Were you a racer?"

"Cars? No, not professionally. But I did a little

barnstorming on some tracks in Wisconsin. Never settled to doing it professionally."

"You drive well," Drew said slowly. "I had a roommate in college from Freedom, Wisconsin. Ever been there?" She held her breath. She could still remember the day the three of them had driven to Madison so that David and Mary Justine could be married.

"Once or twice." *And my godfather's from there. And he sent me looking for you.* The words almost burst from him. He had such an urge to tell her, to open it up, take his chances, convince this woman that he wasn't underhanded, that he wouldn't help anyone—even Justin—to pull the rug out from under her.

Drew had a sinking feeling she should've said nothing. Why open that can of peas? Freedom, Wisconsin. The power of Mary Justine's wealthy father. If he chose, he could fight her for custody of the children. A drawn-out legal battle could wipe out her savings. She had a sudden wish to share her fears with Rex, but innate caution kept her silent.

"Pretty area," Rex murmured, wondering at her withdrawal. He took the plunge, risking a cold insistence that he mind his own business. "Something I can help you with?"

Startled, Drew looked at him warily. "Just . . . just the usual. Will the roof hold? Will the house fall over?"

The powerful car ate up the miles. Rex hung

on grimly to the wheel as they sang round the curves. She was dissembling; she wouldn't let go of her distrust, shed the skin of wariness.

The children loved her. The children had been given to her legally. Rex shook his head. But he would straighten out Justin Drake about his fears for the children. They were doing fine.

"There it is." Drew leaned forward and looked upward through the windshield. "Isn't it wonderful?"

"Yes." Rex had managed a glance to the stately home sitting on the escarpment overlooking what had once been a race-track and was now a New York state park, Taughannock.

"We're awfully early for dinner. Would you like to see the falls?" At his nod she gave directions up the high hill on which the restaurant was built.

Rex was surprised at the steepness of the hill. At the top Drew directed him in a turn past a narrow river roaring with rapids, then down another road to a gravelled parking area. When they got out and walked down the stone steps, he got his first view of the Taughannock Falls. "Wow!" he exclaimed.

Drew chuckled. "Higher than Niagara. Of course, not so wide or grand, but it's ours."

"Impressive."

Fewer than a dozen people milled on the small stone terrace of the overlook. Directly beyond the fence was a good two-hundred-foot drop to the boulder-strewn creek bed that fed into Cayuga Lake.

They were content to listen to the conversations of others.

Rex was pleased because Drew was pressed close to him by the many people in the small space. He kept his arm up near her waist so that he could prevent her being pushed or crowded.

Drew's attention was drawn to the group of senior citizens. For a moment they made her desperately miss her parents. Older than her mother and father would've been, they had the same sparkle to the eyes. One woman in particular seemed to Drew to have a glint of happy devilment in her eyes, but a serene smile on her lips. Drew grinned when the spry senior citizen pushed around some of her peers and stood at the corner of the barrier, looking down into the deep gorge. The high waterfall caught the late-day sun, producing a very personal rainbow. The woman, who was short, craned her neck to see, but she was in a blind spot.

Instinctively, Drew moved toward the woman, to help her find an open spot for viewing.

Rex was about to follow her. When he felt the touch on his arm, he turned to face a smiling elderly lady.

"Excuse me, sir. Do you know the name of the Indians who inhabited this area?"

"I'm not sure. They must've been in the Iroquois Nation—"

"Well, I knew that." She frowned. "I'm not stupid, you know."

"Of course not. But, you see, I'm not from this area—"

"Then why did you answer?" The senior citizen asked spiritedly.

Drew glanced for a moment at Rex, grinning at his predicament, then looked back at the spritely lady. Her grin was swallowed by shock at what she saw. "No," she whispered.

The old woman had moved around the end of the barrier to a small ledge of rock and earth. Her footing was downright perilous, just inches from the two-hundred-foot drop.

"No," Drew said again, her voice anguished. Stones had begun sliding under the woman's feet. It wouldn't take much to cause a slide. Drew knew she mustn't excite the woman.

Legs like lead, arms outstretched, fear roiling her insides, Drew moved. She sensed rather than saw the dirt crumble. The elderly lady tried to arch back against the barrier, her feet and hands clawing for purchase as the slight action made her slide. Her arms lifted, flailing.

Drew leapt, her middle thudding against the barrier, knocking the wind out of her. One desperate clutching hand found the woman's sweater, closing on it, jerking it, praying it was strong material. The pull of the woman's body jackknifed Drew's, and she fought to keep her balance and not follow over the barricade. Below were the rocks and cataracts, the deep pool beneath the falls. She kicked her toes into the stonework, needing a hold.

"Henrietta!"

The screech turned heads. People yelled—some groaned; others squealed.

"Dammit, Drew!" Rex cursed steadily, throwing his body at her as her feet began to leave the ground. The woman's weight had been inching her over the parapet. He gripped one thigh, steadying her, his feet pushing hard into the stone wall, the extra weight acting as a dragging anchor and slamming him hard against the top of the fence. People screeched and shouted around them. "Quiet!" Rex yelled into the clamor.

He swallowed hard. "All right. Listen. Ma'am, stay still. Drew, have you a good grip on her?"

"I . . . I need both hands. Hold me."

"I will." Sweat popped out on his forehead as he gripped both her legs. He knew she was being scratched and abraded by the stone and wood top of the barricade. But he couldn't adjust his grip for fear of losing both of them. She'd take a header down the cliff and be smashed along with the woman. Terror had him clutching her.

"I . . . I have a better grip now."

"Good girl. Look, I'm going to try to maneuver

to the side. Hang on. Don't look around. I'll try to go slow."

Hands came out next to Rex. "I'll help. She's a passenger on my tour bus," a man said shakily.

"Good. Can you get a rope? We need to anchor her. No. Forget it. You can't reach. And we don't need anyone else loose on that ledge. Have someone take hold of your belt. Climb out there . . . slowly. Reach carefully. Maybe you can grab her."

Other men who'd been listening quietly took positions. Firmly held by others, the bus driver climbed the barricade. He hooked the slight woman into his arms, bringing her back.

Rex hauled on Drew, holding her shaking body against him. He tremored with aftermath himself and could only kiss her hair, again and again.

"You're all right," he said repeatedly.

"Thanks to you." She clung to him. "My knees are water."

"Mine aren't much better. So we'll crawl."

"Good butlers think of everything," she laughed shakily.

Voices rose in a cacophony of teary relief and laughter and gratitude.

"That was brave, ma'am. I thank you, and so does my passenger—and she'd tell you that herself, but she's resting. I'm taking her to a doctor." The bus driver shook Drew's hand, and Rex's.

Rex kept his arm around Drew as they walked to the car.

"Your arm is trembling," she told him, her voice quavering.

"I like my job . . . and I almost lost my boss. Unnerving," he said, trying to smile. He'd had such a sense of loss, such an angry river of what might've been, roaring through him when he thought he might not get to her in time. Not all the horror was gone. "I don't want to lose you," he said, shock, awe, and a sense of purpose in his voice.

"Thank you." Heat, gratitude, and a happy lassitude filled her. "I think we're late for our dinner reservation."

"And we're a little messier than we were," he said ruefully, brushing ineffectually at her clothes and his own, wanting to take hold of her thigh again, this time to caress it, to embrace all of her.

"We'll explain?" The heat of his hand came through her clothing. He'd saved her at the risk of his own life. How could she be suspicious of a gallant man like that? Her entire being quivered with the torrid force of his touch. She couldn't afford to be caught up in a relationship that could get out of control . . . and she was sure that could happen. Maybe he was a butler—that was strange enough. But he was no ordinary man, and that made her more than cautious.

Rex noted her fixed look but ignored it, shaking his head. One step at a time. He had to come to terms with knowing that he would've been permanently bereft if anything had happened to her. "No one will believe us."

Smiling tentatively, each caught in tumultuous thought, they reentered the car, driving slowly down the winding Falls road to the highway that fronted on the lake. "Look, albino deer."

Head back against the seat, Drew turned, nodding, feeling the great lassitude that she always experienced after a crisis. "I've seen them up here at other times."

"Did anyone ever tell you your crisis reaction is about a ten?" Rex drawled.

"My reflexes sharpened with motherhood," she muttered. "But my aftermath is horrible. I feel like a wet noodle."

Stopping the car, Rex leaned on the wheel, looking over at her. "You scared me."

"I scared myself." She caught her breath at the hot look in his eyes. "Thank you."

"You've already done that." Almost against his will, he leaned toward her. He watched the myriad expressions of shyness, surprise. "I don't want to lose you." His face was inches from hers.

Confusion roared through her. "We're late," she all but bleated, fumbling with the car door, opening it, and almost falling to the pavement in her hurry to get out. Brushing herself off as well as possible, she hurried across the parking lot and up the porch steps, pausing on the wraparound porch with its gingerbread and trumpet vines to take deep breaths. Then, without looking back to see if Rex was behind, she entered the restaurant.

When the hostess bustled up to her, beaming, Drew was taken aback. "Ah, we're not as well dressed as we were, that is, we're a little messy. Been at the falls—"

"We know, Miss Laughlin. One of the people who witnessed what you did is a guest here. She told us. We've told all the dinner guests of your heroism."

"You have?" Drew said weakly. "How nice." She held back when the beaming woman made a sweeping gesture that she should precede her.

"Better do it," Rex said in her ear. "You're a celebrity."

"Then so are you," she said from the side of her mouth. His chuckle propelled her forward faster than a push would've done. She didn't feel like his employer. She felt girlish and silly, like a teenager on a first date. What power did Rex Dakeland have that he could turn her to jelly?

Ridiculous. She didn't need any more complications than there were in her life. She had enough raising two children . . . and trying to make a living . . . and wondering if Mary Justine's father would ever find them and try to take the children from her.

They were seated with a flourish at a table by the window that had a panoramic view of Cayuga Lake.

"What were you thinking when she ushered us to the table?"

"I was thinking of my children."

"You love them."

"Very much."

His heart squeezed in his chest. "They're wonderful kids." He looked out the window, sipping the ice water poured by the busboy.

Drew followed the direction of his gaze. The lake looked silvery sapphire, with flashes of orange fire as the sun, gloriously setting, preened itself.

"All I could think of when I saw the lady falling was Ira, and how he'd do something like that." Drew shook her head. "Louise isn't as venturesome." She sighed. "Boys."

"We're a wonderful sex."

"You're not a boy."

"Not now, but I was."

"A daredevil."

Rex winced. "A little bit."

"A lot."

Rex frowned at her. "Have you been talking to my mother?"

Drew laughed out loud, causing smiling people to turn their way. All at once she fully realized what she'd done, and life took on luster. She was having a wonderful time. And saving the lovely lady added a brilliant luster.

When the waitress came, they ordered baked sole with capers, fresh tomatoes, and basil.

Drew was amazed at how easily she conversed with Rex. Her early trepidation had vanished. They'd shared a frightening yet most rewarding experience. Saving a life! She felt euphoric now, and she knew without asking that Rex felt the same.

When a champagne chiller was set in the middle of the table and a bottle of Dom Pérignon was twirled in it, Drew gasped, her gaze flying to Rex's. At his negative shrug she looked inquiringly at the waitress.

"The owner sent it over. Everyone's very happy about what you both did," she said simply, smiling at them.

"Thank you," Drew said. When the wine had been poured and the waitress melted away, she smiled at Rex. "I've been saying that all night."

He lifted his glass. "To a very special lady. You've got class." He'd never meant anything more. When she blushed, he chuckled.

She lifted her glass. "To my butler who doesn't look or act like one . . . I don't think. But how would I know? You're the first one I've ever met."

Though she chuckled, Rex glimpsed the wariness deep in her eyes. "Tell me about the children."

She lowered her glass. "Why?"

He shrugged, trying to look bland. He'd touched a nerve. Clumsy! "Just because I think they're special and would like to know more about them."

"Not much to tell," Drew said cautiously. "They were born out of state, and then we moved here."

"You're divorced?"

Drew stared at him, her smile strained. "This is only a night out, not a soul-baring seminar."

"True." Rex backed off. "Tell me about the house."

Drew blinked. "The house?"

"Yes. Most houses have histories, especially those the vintage of yours. Do you know its background?"

She nodded reluctantly. "It's been in my family for a few generations. Not that anyone's lived in it the past ten years until we moved in. My great-grandfather built it and once owned about two hundred acres around it. He was a dairy farmer. There are a great many of them in this state—of course, not as many as there used to be."

"The same in Wisconsin," Rex said, smiling, registering her sudden frown. He waited.

"Have . . . have you ever lived in Madison? I understand it's a nice area."

Rex nodded. "It's a great city, and not just because it's the capital." He forced a smile. "I've been there a few times, always enjoyed it. Never lived there," he told her truthfully. Her almost imperceptible sigh of relief had him awash with guilt. He knew if he told her why he'd come, they might have a chance of talking it over, of keeping the door open. Hell! She didn't have to know. They could build a relationship in New York State. By the time they were good and solid together, he could take her to Wisconsin and—what? Do what? Say what? That he'd been staying in her house under false pretenses. Great. Whatever they had would die a sudden, ugly death. He could picture it.

Drew forked tender fish into her mouth, glancing at him as she did so. She almost choked on the succulent morsel. His twisted features, the sour curve of his mouth, narrowed eyes, frightened her. "What is it? Is your food bad?"

"Used to be allergic to fish as a kid. Haven't eaten any in years, but I don't feel a thing. It should be fine." He scratched his neck with one finger.

Entrées finished, they took the dessert menus, scanning the long list, settling on fresh blueberry pie, served hot with whipped cream on top, a real New York dessert.

Rex rubbed his arm, itching a bit. His neck

felt hot. His throat felt tight, and he was thirsty as hell. Must've been the champagne.

They thoroughly enjoyed the dessert, drinking a great deal of coffee and mineral water with the pie.

Rex pushed away the last of his wine. His throat was downright raspy. His eyes were stinging.

Drew put down her fork; her mouth fell open. "Lord! I can barely see your eyes." She watched his hands cross in front of him, itching both arms, then switching to his neck. "Your allergy," she whispered.

"Naw. Can't be." But he knew it was. He felt hot, disconnected, off center. His breathing was impeded. Damn! This wasn't the time. This was going to be a special evening . . . just the two of them. "I'll get the check," he said hoarsely, trying to lever himself out of the chair.

"No. I'll pay at the outer desk." Taking bills out of her purse, she threw some on the table, then went around to stand next to him when he rose.

"My treat," he said roughly, feeling dizzy.

"Next time. Shall I put my arm around you?"

"No! Lead the way. I'll follow." He followed her, concentrating on putting one foot in front of the other.

In a blur he watched her pay the bill. He wanted to go to her, wrest the check from her hand. Instead he leaned against the antique wall mirror.

Drew threw down the money, watching him over her shoulder. He was sagging! She couldn't take him home like that. Better to take him to the hospital, get an allergy shot. She was closer to the hospital in Ithaca now than she would be if she took him back toward the house and on to Geneva.

Heaving a sigh of relief that the car was just across from the door and not all the way along the garden, she edged him down the shallow steps, one at a time, his knees threatening to buckle at every movement. She propped him against the passenger side and held out her hand. "Keys."

He shook his head ponderously. "I drove you. Take you home."

"You sound like a dying frog." She searched first one pocket then another, felt for the keys, and hit something else.

"Naughty, naughty. Feels nice, though," Rex wheezed soulfully. "Voice must be changing."

"Among other things." How could he react sexually when he was in the midst of an allergy attack?

Getting him into the car was like hoisting a ladle of cooked pasta. Rex had no bones. Drew was red-faced and perspiring by the time she had him in the passenger seat. "You're no lightweight."

"Work out. One eighty-five . . . maybe, six foot three. So's okay . . . I think." He slurred his words. "My mouth's not working."

"Right." Drew got behind the wheel, checking her seat belt and his and studying the dashboard of the car. Despite the vintage, it had a more sophisticated system than anything she'd driven. But she could handle it. She must. After getting it started and driving out of the crowded parking lot, she changed her mind. Twice she stalled because she wasn't used to the stick shift. She laid on the horn when a guest became impatient at her bucking progress and began backing out in front of her. "Take it easy, fella," she called out the window.

"That's tellin' 'em. We'll deck 'em all." Rex coughed, then sighed and put his head back, closing his eyes.

Drew grimaced at him.

The lake road was twisty and narrow enough in daytime. At night it could be a fright. Since she wasn't that confident about her driving in Rex's made-over vintage model, she went slow.

Finally, after a few pullovers and one stall on the hilly, twisting lake road, she curved down the hill leading into Ithaca.

Not even sure she could find her way to the nearest hospital, she drove slower, hoping for a sign. She found one and followed the arrow leading to the emergency room. She drove under the portico, and before the guard could tell her to move, she leaned out the window. "Get me a wheelchair. Fast. Allergic reaction."

In minutes they were in the inner sanctum, and a doctor was giving Rex an injection.

After a time the doctor turned to her. "I think you can take him home. But he'd better rest for a day or so. He's had a pretty strong reaction." He frowned. "Surely he knew . . ."

Drew nodded. "He thought he was past it."

The doctor grimaced. "He isn't. We'll get him to the car for you. He may be pretty groggy when you get him home. Think you can handle him?"

"We'll manage."

On the way home Rex was slumped in his seat, beginning to snore.

It occurred to Drew that she could leave him in the car overnight if she couldn't get him out and in the house.

By the time she turned in the driveway, she'd all but decided on that course of action.

Parking the car as close to the cottage as she could, under the beacon of the carbon lamp she'd installed for night safety, she went around to the passenger side, opened it, and leaned in. When Rex's eyes popped open, she was surprised and immobilized.

"You're beautiful," he said, laughing softly, catching her around the waist and pulling her across his lap, crushing her lips with his.

Stunned, Drew remained flaccid. Her mouth had opened with shock just before he'd closed on it. It couldn't be, she'd never allowed it, she was armored against it. Fear reared in her like a wild mustang. Then, as though she'd given him an invitation, his tongue intruded, caressing hers, teasing, beginning a sexual rhythm that stunned her with its gentle ferocity. Heat rivered through her, yet her skin felt damp and cold as though the fever had given her chills as well. Never had she experienced such a chorus of ambivalent sensations. All of her was on fire; all of her was frozen in place; all of her was vibrating to a brand-new sexual rhythm as old as Adam.

"I want you, Drew." The mellow, sleepy sexiness all but shattered her. No one in her life had said anything so hot to her, so sensuously provocative. Nothing had prepared her for the reactions she'd experienced when Rex had touched her.

"Too quick." The words whistled out of her mouth. Even in the torrid world Rex had carried her to, reason was able to assert itself.

He nuzzled her neck, shifting her on his lap, then groaning at the movement of her backside against him. "You make me so hot, Drew."

"Can't." Helpless, wanting, stunned at her own desires, she tried to push back even as she wanted to embrace him. How did she get in this position? He was sick, for heaven's sake. She trembled from head to toe when he nibbled on her neck. Insane. Not even as a teenager had she enjoyed necking in a car. Now here she was, a grown woman with children, sprawled across a man's lap.

"Sure we can." He grinned at her, then kissed her lingeringly, openly carnal.

Drowning in sensation, Drew collapsed against him, molding her body to his, feeling his hardness, the pulsing need that matched her own. All that wet heat steamed them, spiraling them up and onto another plateau of desire.

When she felt his fingers run up her leg, under her skirt, his hands pressing against the juncture of her body, she bowed taut. Her eyes snapped open, and she looked into his lazily sexual ones. Then somehow she pushed back, almost tumbling out of the car in her haste. Clothes awry, she spun away from the car, streaked into the house, running from Rex, escaping the sexual net of his hands and mouth.

Four

Rex opened his eyes and groaned, his head doing a voodoo dance, the sunlight in his room painful and stabbing. What the hell had happened? His mouth tasting metallic, his tongue thick, he knew he'd had something. Liquor? Medication. Why?

Slowly, the evening came back to him. The lady at the falls, his own foolhardiness in eating fish. It didn't always happen, but he'd known he could be sensitive to it, though most of the time his biggest problem had been with scallops or shrimp. Last night he'd had a reaction. He'd been groggy, nauseated. They'd gone to a hospital. He didn't recall anything after the shot. How the hell had she got him into the car? Into the house?

He crawled from bed and staggered to the tiny bathroom with its rattly, uncertain plumbing.

He eyed himself in the mirror and winced. He looked as though he'd been on a binge.

He couldn't recall getting out of the car or going to bed. But the dreams . . . they were something. And he wouldn't forget them in a hurry. Living color. With Drew. He could still feel her lips, her beautiful breasts. He closed his eyes against a sudden sharp headache and saw her in his mind's eye. Beautiful. Warm. Sexy. What would she think if she knew he'd dreamed of cuddling her in his lap, making love to her in a car?

Stepping into the shower, he let cool water sluice his body while he gasped and groaned. He willed his pounding head to cease its drumbeat, his puffy, achy body to snap back to normal.

Twenty minutes later he was almost ready to face the world. It hurt to turn his head, and his eyes felt burned from the inside out, but he was on his feet and only swaying slightly.

He had ten minutes to get to the big house and start breakfast for Ira and Louise. They were supposed to return late last night, sleep at the neighbors', and get home early for breakfast. They were starting summer camp today, and a bus would pick them up at the house.

He muttered to himself all the way across the lawn and through the back door, the summer kitchen, then the kitchen proper.

When he heard the giggles and not quite

muffled laughter coming from the kitchen, he winced and braced himself, his eyes closing for a moment. They'd aced him. Beaten him to the kitchen. It was his job as butler to get the house moving in the morning. Could he face them? His throbbing head had his teeth aching. Oh, well. No turning back. He stepped through the open doorway into the great room and stared.

Drew was at the stove . . . cooking oatmeal from the smell of it. Ira was making toast. Louise was taking things out of the fridge and putting them on the table. The silverware was a little cockeyed, but Louise had done a pretty good job of setting the table.

"Did Rex throw up?" Louise asked, putting the container of homemade raspberry jam on the table.

Rex braced himself, trying not to dwell on her words. His topsy-turvy stomach was heaving enough to do just that.

"I don't think so, love, but he was very sick. . . ." Drew's voice trailed off, and she gazed out the kitchen window pensively.

"Why?"

"Mom told ya, Louise. It's like getting sick from a shot or something. He can't take it," Ira said matter-of-factly.

Rex winced as the evening came back to him in living color. Fish. He felt like a wimp. At any other place and time, in front of anyone else, he would've laughed. He was confident about himself, knew who he was. He was sure of his place on the planet. But with Drew, with these two kids, it was different. He wanted to be Superman, Robin Hood, and King Richard the Lionhearted all rolled into one, and he didn't even try to question why. It'd been growing from the first day. Love. He loved all three. Pain stabbed behind his eyes, and he groaned. Damn their morning cheer.

Ira turned first at the low sound. "Gee, Rex, we woulda fed you in bed. Right, Louise?"

Louise nodded shyly.

"Thanks, guys. But I'm the butler. And I'm not letting you have my job," Rex said, gritting his teeth against the headache that merely walking across the kitchen had exacerbated. "Coffee," he said hoarsely, looking at Drew and smiling ruefully. When her face reddened and she looked away from him, biting her lip, the smile disappeared from his face. Opening his mouth to ask what had happened, he was stopped by a hand on his arm. By the time he finished answering all of Ira's eager questions, the awkward moment had slipped away.

He moved through the chores head down, gulping black coffee in between runs from the stove to the table. Drew seemed to be on her feet as much as he was.

In short order the children were breakfasting, insisting he join them. He picked at the oatmeal, but drank quarts of black coffee.

The bus came for day camp, and the two children barreled out the door, lunch boxes in hand, knapsacks on their backs.

The house turned silent, serene. Alonzo swished and slapped his way to his sunny spot in the great room. The dog found another close by.

Crack. Squeak. The house had its own language, which resounded in the stillness.

Drew whirled around from the sink. "I would like you to finish out the month and leave. I'll pay you two weeks severance as—"

"What? Why?"

Stunned, Drew glared at him. "That you can ask such a question shows me you're not the person I want around my children."

They're not your children. He was tempted to say it, but he didn't. Both of them having tantrums would be counterproductive, but he couldn't stem the rise of anger inside him. "Something about last night," he said flatly. He lifted his unfinished orange juice and tipped it down his throat, trying to envision the previous evening. He recalled the reaction, the shot. And he'd been drinking champagne. He stood behind her as she banged at the dishes and silverware in the sink. "Leave the dishes. That's my job. And for that matter, get out of my kitchen. I guess we both have work to do." He glared at her when she started to retort.

Long minutes passed as they eyed each other like contenders.

Drew shrugged. "All right. But maybe you should go."

"What the hell for?" He felt guilty, angry, frustrated. And he damn well didn't know why.

She put her nose in the air, outraged. "Maybe if you weren't so irresponsible, you wouldn't have to ask."

"Dammit, Drew—"

"I'm going to work." She sailed out of the room before he could detect the tears on her cheeks; her heart was hammering in her chest. She rushed to her study, slammed the door behind her, and leaned against it. Bowled over by him, she'd responded to him fully, more than she'd ever done with anyone else, and he could pass it off as nothing, not even worth mentioning. Swine! She'd get him out of her life. A butler! Who needed such an archaic thing? She'd come within a hair of letting him make love to her. She'd wanted it badly. Eyes closing for a moment, she tried to shut out the image of herself cuddled in his arms, the way she'd turned into him, compelled by passion, wanting him. How could he not feel the same? No one could forget such electric moments. Her eyes snapped open. The medication. Could he have forgotten? Lord! She shivered with embarrassment. That had to be it. Before she could change her mind, she marched back to the kitchen.

Rex watched her warily. "Drew, listen to me—"

"Forget what I said. You can stay." Hot with the humiliation that she was the only one who recalled those torrid moments in the car, she spun on her heel and almost ran back to her office.

For the rest of the morning she hammered away at a satiric piece aimed at pointing up the injustice of men being paid more than women for the same work. At a stopping place, she leaned forward and put her head in her hands.

Last night had been nothing to him. How could it have been? He knew nothing of it. How could she have let him get so close? She'd sworn she'd never let her guard down again with anyone. Stabbed with rejection, she stifled a moan. She felt weak and unprotected. He'd lifted her to a new plane of sensual awareness. She'd quivered with the realization of how passionate she could be. Maybe it was just as well he didn't recall anything. It might be easier on her when he left if the whole matter was just an interlude that only she remembered. She couldn't handle it if she fell more deeply in love with him.

Love? Had that happened? Groaning, she almost fell off her swivel chair in her rush to the bathroom. Then she spent the next several minutes splashing cold water on her face. Entering her adjoining bedroom, she dragged off her clothes and yanked a tank suit from the drawer. She'd worn this kind of suit when she'd swum in competition. She needed a hard, fast workout now to chase away anxiety. Pulling some summer sweats over her suit, she grabbed her goggles and cap.

Going down the front staircase, she paused on the right-angle landing and looked down into the foyer. Two workmen were there! What was going on? How the hell had Rex had such audacity—and such push that he'd gotten men here in the few hours since breakfast?

"I didn't think the jacking would work. It did. That could've been an expensive operation if it hadn't held."

"You should know that Rex has the eye. When he says that's where to put it, that's what we do. Let's go down and check the flooring. We might need to nail and reglue in some places."

Their voices faded as they strolled to the kitchen and down the stairs to the cellar. What had they meant? Did they know Rex? How long had he been in the area? Suspicion mushroomed inside her. She felt threatened, violated, invaded.

Wiping moist hands on her pants, she went down to the foyer and headed out the front door to the half-wraparound porch. When Rex came out another door, her gaze sharpened on him.

Wariness assailed him at her look. "Now what?"

"The workers. And don't say you don't know them."

"I won't."

Startled at the disclosure, though somehow she'd been sure he wouldn't lie to her, she stared at him. "How long have you been in this area?"

"About a month. But I've been to New York many times. Mostly Manhattan," he told her abruptly.

Chin in the air, she stared at him. It made her dizzy to look in his eyes, but she didn't flinch. "I see."

"The bulk of the renovation will take time." What was she thinking? He felt he was walking on eggs with her.

"Bulk?" Head whirling, she stared at him. "Jacking up the floors. That's all." When he shook his head, a cash register went off in her head. "I don't want any more than that." She couldn't afford even that!

Rex shook his head. "Can't be helped. There'll be cracks in the walls that'll need plastering. Permanent jacks have to be installed. The grouting on the basement walls needs redoing. Some windows will have to be replaced—"

"What? We discussed this yesterday. I said no, Rex. No!"

"—because the cost of heating will skyrocket if you don't. The roof has to be checked, inside and out, so does the plumbing—"

"Good Lord, can't you hear? Are you out of your mind?"

Rex hesitated. "All right. Renovating old homes was a hobby of mine that turned from a hobby into a business. If you agree to let me show the house as an example of my work, we'll call it square."

"That's stretching, and you know it! And why are you pretending to be my butler?"

He stared at her. "I was in the area, saw the house. It intrigued me. Italianate villas of this vintage are gems." That much was true. He'd loved the house on sight.

"But your business must need you. This is the best season for construction work," she said slowly.

"True." He took a breath and told her the truth. "But I'd counted on a big contract coming through. It didn't." It probably would in the fall. He didn't tell her that. Damn Justin. Tell the truth—that he'd come East just to meet her and her family, size them up, give a report—and she'd throw him out.

"I . . . I think you're dissembling," she blurted.

"Lying, you mean." He hitched a shoulder against one of the long shutters that edged the floor-to-ceiling windows. "If you were a man, I'd sock you for saying that."

"If I were a man, you would've been more up-front with me." With that she spun around and sprinted down the front steps.

At the dock she got out of her sweats, ran to the end of the board, and sprang outward in a clean, hard dive that took her into deep water. The dash of coldness was like a salve to her raveled nerves, and she swam straight out, stroking hard, needing the crisp edge of coldness that the clear water gave her.

It did no good to tell herself that she didn't know Rex, that he presented danger merely by his evasiveness. She'd known him from the beginning of time, had seen his face in all her dreams, wanted him from before childhood. Damn his eyes!

Diving down in a sinuous motion, she wove among the eelgrass and thin layer of weeds that fed the fish and hid their spawn. The world was special under water. No noise, no problems, no Rex. She'd always been able to hold her breath longer than anyone on her swimming teams. It'd been a knack she'd had since childhood. Now she strung it out to the fullest, welcoming the longing for air . . . stretching . . . stretching . . .

The hands closing like a vise around her waist startled her into opening her mouth, swallowing lake water. She shot to the surface all but jackknifed by the person holding her. Coughing, choking, bending her head back to get air, she couldn't speak.

"What the hell happened? Are you out of your mind going out so far?"

Rex was able to tread water and shake her at the same time. "Dammit, you could've drowned. What if I hadn't been here? You don't go swimming alone again!"

Drew stared at him. Anger, frustration, fueled her spasm of coughing, and she couldn't get words out. She struggled with him, trying to get one hand free so she could belt him. The ham-handed idiot had made her swallow half of Cayuga Lake.

"Stop, stop. I've got you. I won't let you go." Rex tried to soothe her until he got a look at her furious expression. "Hey! What gives? Oh, never mind. I'll get you out of here first."

To add to her ire, he began towing her in, his arm under her breast. Since she knew that struggling at that point would fill her mouth with water again, she stayed motionless, trying to control her coughing.

When her feet touched the stony bottom of the lake, she stood, banging his chest with her hands to free herself.

"Take it easy, Drew. Let me get you out—"

"I'll get out myself, thank you. And for your information"—she coughed—"I didn't need help. I've set records for staying under water, and I've done it for years." She climbed up the ladder and grabbed her towel.

Rex swung up and stood in front of her.

For the first time she noticed he was clad in

jeans, no shirt, without shoes. The denim clung to his legs and waist, outlining his manliness, drawing her eyes. "You . . . you thought I was drowning."

"Damn straight. How the hell was I to know you swim under water like a fish? Hell, Drew, you don't tell me anything."

She ignored his chagrin, the obvious trembling of his hands as he dragged them through his hair. "There's a lot of that going around," she told him shakily.

Tautly angry, he stared at her, reading the message in her eyes. "I admit there are things I should tell you," he said softly, his smile twisted. "But even if I told you the truth, you wouldn't listen to me."

"That's admitting that you've been lying to me."

"No. I haven't told you everything, but I've tried not to lie to you."

"Have you succeeded?" That he could dash her dreams, turn her hopes to vinegar . . . Damn his soul.

Rex saw her stiffen. "What?"

"Are you after my children?" She edged toward the built-in bench on the dock, the shovel and rake leaning there.

Rex glanced from her to the bench, comprehending her action. He moved quickly, pinioning her arms at her sides. "Now wait a minute. Please."

"I won't let you hurt them, I won't," Drew said through her teeth, grief, fury, horror, mixing into a blistering resistance to anything he might say.

"Dammit, I wouldn't!"

"Then what is going on? You know the workmen, you've been in this state longer than you said—"

"I told you when I came from Wisconsin, before I got a job as your butler. That's true. I also told you that I've been to New York before, but mostly it's been to New York City, on business."

"Did you seek us out?" His hesitation was answer enough. She flung herself at the rake, grabbed, and swung back toward him, readying to strike.

"Hey, Rex! What the hell's going on?"

The workman's voice made them both freeze in place.

"Nothing, Gabe. Everything's fine. Go on back to work."

"Okay. Just wanted to tell you that we've nailed up a few boards, need to replace some."

Rex nodded, not taking his eyes from Drew. "Do it."

Drew snapped out of her near hypnotic state. "No. No more expense. I won't allow it."

Gabe gaped at her. "But, Mrs. Laughlin, it's all been factored in on the original price."

"Which is?" Drew braced herself. She saw the infinitesimal glance from Gabe to Rex, then he shrugged. "Tell me," she said through her teeth.

"I . . . I can't give you an exact figure, ma'am, but when I get back to the house, I'll get the estimate and put it on your desk."

"Do that," Drew said tautly, trying not to shiver. She strode toward the end of the jetty, intending to walk up the short hill to the road rather than climb the boathouse steps.

"Listen to me," Rex said to her back.

"Talk, then," she answered him quickly, not turning.

"Not like this. Can't we discuss this tonight after dinner, when the children are in bed?"

"That bad, huh?" She tried to ignore the trickle of regret, the stream of grief, that assailed her.

"No. But you have to listen . . . and try to understand."

"I'll listen. Now I have to change." Shudders racked her from head to toe.

"You're cold."

"A little." Mostly it was shock, deprivation, sorrow. If only he hadn't meant so much.

Rex watched her go up the hill, swathed in her towel, wrapped against the chill, buffered against him. It was like saying good-bye. Grim-lipped, he marched into the boathouse, frowning at the phone there. For two cents he'd go out and buy one for the cottage. He lifted the old-fashioned phone and placed his call. The phone rang four times. Just before the message machine went on, someone answered.

Rex recognized the smoke-roughened voice. If Justin had quit smoking earlier than last year, that hoarseness might've been gone from his voice by now. "The game's up. She knows some of it. I'm explaining the rest after dinner tonight. What happens then is up to you." Rex paused. "I have a stake in the game now, and I'm going to do everything I can to protect it."

"Rex! No. Don't tell her everything. . . ."

"Everything. Tonight. I'm not going to lose because you want to play cat-and-mouse—"

"You know it's more than that."

"Then be up-front. No more games. Everything is on the line. Incidentally, the kids couldn't be better. They're smart, eager, and crazy about their mother."

"All right. We'll do it your way. And I'm glad the children are fine." There was a long pause. "I suppose I've always known it had to come to this. Maybe I've been too afraid." He coughed. "I could use a cigarette . . . but before you harp on it, I'll tell you that I won't smoke. I guess there's no more to say. I'll be flying East as soon as I can get a flight. I'll stay in that bed-and-breakfast you mentioned. Can you get me a reservation?"

"I'll call," Rex said abruptly, not sure his life wouldn't be over after dinner but determined.

"You're angry."

"I'm furious, Justin. I have a hell of a lot to lose in this charade of yours." He paused. "And I know some of it's my fault for not chucking the whole thing at the outset and telling the truth."

"She'd never have let you in the house."

"And now she may turn her back on me, and I'll lose it all." He squeezed his eyes shut at the sudden wrenching pain.

"You love her," Justin said, shock in his voice.

"Good-bye." Rex slammed down the phone, staring at the slats and two-by-fours in the unfinished room above the boat hoist. Love? Dammit to hell. How'd she do that to him? No matter how she struggled, he wasn't going to give her up without a fight. And he'd tell her so.

Drew was glad the children were there, noisy, boisterous, demanding her full attention and concentration. She'd forgotten that Ira and Louise's friends would be coming to dinner. Four extra mouths to feed, happy, bouncy bodies to watch, needs to be seen to. She could ignore Rex . . . for a while.

Rex had seen Drew leaning on the high

counter that separated the kitchen area from the rest of the great room. Her stare, her fixation, her concentration, had all pierced him like sharp hooks. What had she been thinking? How to get rid of him, how to turn her back, forget he ever existed? She could try. But he damn well wasn't going to let her. He had waited a lifetime for something he hadn't even known existed, and he wasn't about to go down without a fight. She'd know it all before he was through, not just about Justin, but how he felt. He'd been on a search and never knew it, a quest that had no name. But he'd found the prize, and nothing and no one were going to wrest it from him, even the "prize" herself: Drew.

Dinner was chaotic, loud, and filled with childish laughter. Macaroni-and-cheese was scarfed down; the salad had mixed reviews; the gelatin, raves; the ice-cream sundaes with berries, a standing ovation.

Too soon, parents came for the visitors. There were long good-byes.

Louise and Ira were exhausted.

"I'll carry Louise. You go up and make sure her pj's are ready," Rex told Drew.

"Wear nigh'gown," Louise said into his neck.

"Sorry about that, love."

"I love you, too, Rex."

Stricken, Drew swung around on the landing, looking from the almost-sleeping child to Rex's expressionless face. "This doesn't change anything," she whispered.

"It hasn't for me," he shot back in a low voice. "I've loved her from the moment I first saw her."

Fuming, Drew glared at him. "You know I didn't mean that."

"Well, I do." He nudged past her on the landing and strode up to the children's bedroom.

The usual blackmail of stories, drinks, and questions prolonged the good nights. But soon both children were down in their respective rooms, and lights were out.

Rex preceded Drew down the stairs, going directly to the kitchen and pulling out a liter of mineral water. Filling two glasses with ice, lime slices, and a dash of bitters, he poured the sparkling water to the top. When he turned around with the two brimming glasses, she was there. "Thought you might be thirsty. It's a warm night."

"So it is." Turning, she moved stiffly to the lounge area of the great room, switched on a low lamp, and sat down on the sagging couch. She took the drink reluctantly, then watched as he sat down opposite her. "I told you I'd listen. I didn't say it would affect the outcome."

"No, you didn't say that." Rex sipped the sharp liquid, needing its sting, wishing it were Glenlivet, a double.

"You came here about the children." Even as

she said it, she prayed he'd deny it, deny and convince her of her foolhardiness.

Rex looked up at her. "Yes." When she gasped and leaned back as though struck, he realized she'd been hoping for a denial. "I won't lie to you," he said hoarsely, wanting to go to her, hold her, reassure her. She looked as if he'd punched her.

"You already have," she whispered, scrambling backward on the sofa as though to be farther from him. "I won't let you take them."

Her tortured whispers tore at him. He shook his head. "I wouldn't. I didn't come to do that."

"Justin Drake sent you, didn't he?"

"Yes."

"He can't have them. It's too late. They're mine. What kind of person are you that you'd do his dirty work?"

"Justin's my father's oldest friend. I knew Mary Justine . . . but not well. Justin adored her, then they had a falling-out. It broke his heart when she and her husband died." Rex shook his head, his lips tight. "He wants to see his grandchildren."

"It would crucify me to lose them." Tears threatened to spill over. She bit her lip.

Rex shook his head. "I can't believe he'd try to hurt you. He's a good man."

"I know he was once. But he hurt Mary Justine and David," Drew said vehemently. "He wouldn't recognize how much in love they were. It wasn't fitting that a daughter of his marry a starving artist. When they had the children, he wanted them to come back to Wisconsin. He offered to put David in his firm. They didn't want that. Instead David found a position as an art instructor at the University of Chicago. I was working there. They stayed with me until they found their own place in the same building. The three of us were always together." Drew bit back a sob. "Then, a little over a year ago, they were killed. One dark night. One drunk driver. And they were gone. It was their wish I raise their children if anything happened to them. No one thought it would come to that, but I have proof of their wishes, and I'll fight any attempt of Justin's to take them. I've adopted them legally as their parents wished. And that's all there is to it!" She leapt up and ran from the room.

Five

In bed Rex struggled with the growing sensation that life would be a void without Drew and the children.

His head ached, a leftover from the allergy attack. Now he lay with his arm over his face, trying to force sleep.

Nothing came but fragmented pictures. Bizarre visions. He was holding Drew on his lap, kissing her; their mouths were open, tongues entwined. He'd had that same dream the night before. But now he was awake, and the images were even sharper. How could he think of such things when he'd just had a confrontation with Drew? And knowing Justin would be in town soon, and that his arrival would exacerbate all the raw feelings between them, made him squirm and shift.

Then he saw Drew again in his mind's eye,

clear as a bell. She was across his lap, his body hardening under hers, the want deepening to a wildly arousing moment that couldn't be forgotten—

Stunned, he shot to a sitting position, his arm flying off his face. It wasn't a dream! It had happened. The damned medication! It had made him crazy . . . and stupid. How could he think he dreamed such a thing? Fool! He jumped out of bed, naked, angry, upset, aroused. She'd responded like the dream, the way he'd wanted her to, the way he'd needed. Grabbing a pair of jeans, he hauled them on, then flung himself out the door, across the lawn, and through the big house. A step squeaked, making him pause. He didn't want to awaken the children, perhaps frighten them. He took deep breaths.

In the upper hall he stared long at Drew's bedroom door. There was a movement to his right. Alonzo! "Sorry, old man, I haven't time for you right now. But you're not supposed to be up here." He was getting used to the lizard and had to admit he had an elusive charm. He'd have to remember to take Alonzo downstairs.

Drew's door was slightly ajar. Another deep breath and Rex pushed it open, shut it behind him, and crossed to her bed.

She was lying on her stomach. Staring at her he found an erotic pleasure beyond his dreams. He wanted her with more than passion. He wanted her fastened to his life, a part of him like his lips, his heart. He wanted to wake up with her, go to sleep with her, talk with her, argue with her, yell at her and let her yell back. No. Justin wouldn't be allowed to interfere with that. Even if Drew tried, he'd fight, tooth and claw. His life was on the line. And she and the children were that life.

Bending down, he slipped in beside her. There wasn't the room he needed since it was a double bed—not the king-size his stature demanded—too short, too narrow. He was content. Her heat warmed him. He moved closer, until her body was almost touching his, and closed his eyes. This was reality, not the fantasy some people believed love was, just the wonderful, hot, hard-core reality of need. Sleep came like a visiting wraith, stealthy, quiet. Rex curled into the heat and knew he'd need it for a lifetime.

Hours later Drew opened her eyes, inhaling the gentle, coolish breeze coming in the window, loving the scents of predawn, one sleepy barn owl sounding a call. Stretching into more sleep, she turned, her eyes opening sleepily before she'd slip deeper into slumber.

A strangled sound of outrage penetrated Rex's peaceful dreams. One eyelid peeled upward, reluctantly, then the other. "Hi, beauti-

ful. Your mouth's open." He stretched toward
her to kiss her. When she reared back, surprised ire stretching her features taut, he
shrugged. "Why've you got the sheet up to your
neck that way?" he asked on a mighty yawn.
His mouth dropped shut, and he ground his
teeth. "Looks silly. Stop frowning. Start the day
with a smile." He tried to show her one, but
another yawn interrupted it. He sat up, trying
to see her clock. Damn dark outside. "Morning,
Drew. Am I late?" He blinked. "Can't be. It's
dark out. Go to sleep."

"Out!" She pushed at him; but the sheet
covering her slipped, and she had to grab for it.

Rex leaned back and put his hands behind
his head, staring at her in the near darkness,
seeing her tense outline. "Calm down, love.
You'll get an acid stomach."

"Get out!"

"Don't raise your voice. You'll wake the children." He studied her intently. "I know."

"What do you think you know?" Drew said
through her teeth, edging toward the side of the
bed.

"It wasn't a dream. All this time I thought it
was. You knew it too."

Drew froze. "You're rambling. Leave."

"After we returned from the hospital, my
loving you was real, wasn't it?" He could see
and feel her stiffen. "Don't try to deny it. That's
why you looked at me so strangely in the morn-

ing, why you blushed, why you looked so hurt—"

"I wasn't hurt," she blurted.

"Were too." He pushed up on his elbows so that his face was close to hers. "It was wonderful, and you thought I'd passed it off. If I'd had any idea it was real, I'd have been in your bed before now."

"Get out," she whispered.

"No. Not until you know how I feel."

"I won't listen. I'll leave."

"I'll follow."

"You came here under false pretenses."

"True. But I'm staying for other reasons. I like you. No, more than that. I want to arm-wrestle with you over who walks the dog. I want to tussle with you over who does the grocery shopping—"

"Stop it," she said hoarsely.

"I won't, and I'm not going away, because I can't. You'll have to get an army to drag me away from you. I'm sticking. I want you and the children forever, Drew. You'll have to deal with that, aye or nay. That's your problem. I know my future. If yours is different, you deal with it. I'm not leaving you."

"Good Lord," she whispered, her body sagging down to the mattress. "How can you talk like that? Is this another scam? Another way to trick me?"

"No. I'm staying with you for life. I need you

and the children. You can figure it out in the next fifty years. I might not ever be able to, but I'm not fooling. I'm in for the long haul. Slice, dice, pare, and peel—whatever you have to do to figure it out, you do it. I'm set. But no matter what you decide, I'll be here. You'll be seeing me every day, so feel free to ask any questions that come to mind."

"You betrayed me," she said, feeling queasy and confused.

"No. I did a favor for a friend. It involved subterfuge, yes, but I didn't betray you, because I didn't know you, and didn't know I'd love and respect you. And to set the record straight, I'd made up my mind the first day that I'd do nothing to hurt you."

"But you did."

He reached for her, but she pulled back. He sighed and sank back against the pillows. "I was hoping you'd trust me. I want to go into Rochester to see a ball game with you and the kids tonight. It's Saturday. Will you let me take you?" The room was lightening with a predawn silver, and he saw her narrow-eyed skepticism. "I suppose you wouldn't let me take them unless you were along, even if I wanted it that way, and I don't."

"Right." She plucked at the sheet swathed around her body. "Won't Justin be coming? You'll have to see him and tell him it's no deal."

Rex shrugged. "He has a place to stay. I can

FREE — EXCLUSIVE ROMANCE NOVEL
RISK-FREE PREVIEW —
6 LOVESWEPT NOVELS!

- NO OBLIGATION
- NO PURCHASE NECESSARY

REMEMBER!

- The free gift is mine to keep!
- There is no obligation!
- I may preview each shipment for 15 days!
- I may cancel anytime!

(DETACH AND MAIL CARD TODAY.)

BUSINESS REPLY MAIL

FIRST CLASS MAIL   PERMIT NO. 2456   HICKSVILLE, NY

POSTAGE WILL BE PAID BY ADDRESSEE

LOVESWEPT
BANTAM DOUBLEDAY DELL DIRECT
PO BOX 985
HICKSVILLE   NY   11802-9827

NO POSTAGE
NECESSARY
IF MAILED
IN THE
UNITED STATES

see him tomorrow." His lips tightened. "I think you should give him that message."

She gasped. "No. I don't want to talk to him."

"And I won't be your messenger." He sighed. "Look, I'm going to be around, in your life. A great deal needs straightening out. Why don't we do it a step at a time?"

Drew had the surreal sensation that her life was a carousel, whirling faster and faster. How could they carry on such a conversation when they were in bed, aware of each other, fighting each other? Absurd.

All at once Rex grabbed her and pulled her over his lap, the sheet rumpling to her waist, his eyes lazily going over her small but full breasts that tilted so tantalizingly toward his mouth. "This is the way it was that night."

"No," she said weakly.

"Don't lie, Drew. We didn't go much further, but it was sexy and beautiful." He didn't refuse the invitation of those rosebud nipples but took one into his mouth, sucking gently. Then he gave the same undivided attention to the other, his mouth moving lazily over her skin. "Ummn, you taste so sweet in the morning." He kissed her long, searchingly, desire flaring in both of them.

Drew was deposited back on her side of the bed so quickly, she blinked, openmouthed at a very aroused Rex who was now standing next to her bed, looking down at her, his eyes hot.

"Yes, my darling, I'd like nothing more than to climb back in there again, make love to you for a day and a half, kiss your whole body from chin to toe and back again . . . but I can't. Have to make oatmeal," he told her cheerily, striding out the door, naked, and whistling.

Hot, bothered, rumpled, she lay panting, not quite sure what had happened. She cursed him roundly, devising all manner of painful demises for him. Then she fell back, exhausted. "Damn his butlering hide." Drew groaned and turned on her stomach, pushing her face into the pillow. "Oatmeal?"

She felt slightly less rocky after a long shower. But she was still muttering to herself when she entered the kitchen.

"Hi, Mommy. We're going to Rochester to see baseball. Rex says," Louise said, her eyes shining. "And we have a car with a bed in the back. We can sleep. Nice."

Ira nodded, his mouth full of fruit and oatmeal.

Drew's dicta about how they couldn't do this, they wouldn't do that, died aborning. She couldn't shut down that wonderful gleam, that happy anticipation.

"And I'll be able to see everything because we have good seats, Rex says. Rex says we won't take our animals this time," Ira explained helpfully.

Drew smiled weakly. "No. They don't like baseball."

Ira frowned. "Funny, huh?"

"Very," Drew concurred, not even able to summon up a scowl when she looked at a beaming Rex.

"Oatmeal," Rex said, smiling sweetly as he set the heaping, steaming bowl in front of her.

"I don't think . . ." Drew's voice trailed when she saw how intently the children watched her. "Maybe just a little." It wouldn't do to refuse to eat when she touted oatmeal to them so often.

"I like Rex's oatmeal. It isn't lumpy." Ira beamed at Drew, blithely unaware of the back-hander he'd just served her.

"Good." Rex grinned. "Cooking oatmeal will be my job until you go to college. By then you should've learned how to do it on your own."

Ira looked thoughtful, then nodded. "Okay."

Louise nodded, too, her milk mustache stretching in a semicircle.

Drew, confused and off balance, said nothing.

"Fine. We're agreed on that. Now let's do our chores, so we can be ready to go by noon. We'll eat on the road, take our time—"

"It's under a two-hour drive," Drew said limply. "We needn't go until. . . " Her voice trailed at the rampant disappointment on three faces. She focused on the eldest of the three. "Why Rochester? Syracuse is closer."

"That team is playing out of town," he explained. "And driving in slowly would give the children a chance to sightsee. I've booked a hotel room, so that if they're too tired, we can stay over until morning."

"Rex—"

"Please," Ira said softly.

Louise's eyes widened to plate size.

Drew capitulated with a weary nod, feeling surrounded and outgunned. "Play ball."

Rochester, like the rest of the state, sweltered in summer heat.

"I got rooms overlooking the river," Rex told her as he pulled into the underground garage.

"How many?"

"A suite consisting of two bedrooms and a sitting room in between. Two baths."

"You're not hurting for money."

The tightness in her voice reached him. "I didn't take any money from Justin for coming East, Drew, if that's what you mean." He glanced over his shoulder. The two in back were gawking at the sights. "In fact, I lost money on the deal."

"I can't dredge up any sympathy." But it was harder and harder to throw up barriers to him. Rex had gotten under her skin. She doubted he could be removed, even surgically.

"I'll try and make it up later in the year," he said abruptly. He pulled up to the side door of the hotel and got out of the car, directing the luggage to two attendants, then striding ahead into the lobby.

"I like baseball," Louise said at her side.

"You've never seen any," Ira said practically.

"But I know I'll like it," Louise answered with the firm logic of the young.

"I'm sure you will," Drew muttered, wondering how she was going to get out of the web tightening around her. Rex was taking over her life. In a short time he'd be gone, and she'd have to deal with that pain. Why did he insist on making it worse by an outing like this? Damn his hide.

After they were settled and the children had eaten and insisted they weren't tired, Rex took them to the Woodbury Museum in the center of town, famous for its rare and extensive collection of dolls. Even Ira was entranced with them. From there they went to the Eastman House, the mansion that once had belonged to the founder of the Kodak company and was now a well-known museum of photography. That, too, was located in the city on a beautiful wide avenue of grand homes.

By the time they returned, the children were ready for a nap.

Rex stared at her when Drew returned to the sitting room. "We can talk about one thing or another. I'd like to discuss when we came home from the hospital—"

"Tell me about Justin."

Rex backed off immediately. "I've always cared for him. He's a gentle man. But he lives with an overpowering guilt about his daughter."

Drew sighed. "Mary Justine loved her father. But she was as stubborn as he." She shook her head. "So sad. I'm sure they would have reconciled. But now he wants to see his grandchildren. And I'm afraid of a hidden agenda."

Rex didn't pretend to misunderstand. "I don't think there is one. He's suffering from regret. A sense of his own mortality. A need to connect up with the only family he has." He shrugged. "I'm sure that's what it is."

"It seems I've had them a lifetime."

Rex nodded. "I understand. But if you could've seen Justin when he found out that they'd died, that his grandchildren had been taken away. Everyone in my family was sure he'd die too."

"I had the feeling he didn't search for them." Drew looked away from him. "I put out feelers of my own, so I know. With some of the insurance money I had our lawyer hire detectives to see if anyone was looking in Wisconsin or in the Chicago area for the children. They found no trace." She swallowed, caught between pity and bitter wariness. "I guess I was lulled into a false sense of security."

Rex shook his head. "I think he was dealing with the shock of Mary Justine's and her husband's deaths." He hurt for her, for the fear and anger she tried to hide. I won't let anyone hurt you, he told her silently.

Can I trust you? "I'm afraid."

"He wants to talk to you. No one is going to hurt you, or them." Rex rose to his feet, approaching her chair so quickly and fluidly that she didn't have time to react. Kneeling in front of her, he put his hands along the arms of her chair, blocking her. "I want to talk to you about us, Andrew Laughlin."

"There's nothing to say." But she wanted to blurt, "Tell me this is no game, Rex, tell me that." Pain formed a huge lump in her throat. Agony was smarting in her eyes.

"Yes, there is," he said gently. "You're not the only one who's been cut adrift by what's happened—"

"Ridiculous." Could he see her soul? Damn Rex. His slow, lopsided smile made goose bumps rise on her skin.

He shook his head. "You feel something for me, Drew, and I feel a hell of a lot for you. I don't want an affair. I want a lifetime, a commitment, time to know you. And that might take fifty years." He leaned forward and kissed her nose.

"I . . . I don't know if I can trust you." But she did trust him. And trust had grown by itself, without any feeding from her. Even if she hated him, she knew instinctively she could trust him, and could trust the children with him.

That was an insane amalgam of emotions. "You didn't hurt Alonzo or Faulkner," she said simply.

Factoring that slice of information, he shook his head slowly, knowing she'd paid him the ultimate compliment. "Thank you. No, ma'am, I wouldn't hurt the least of your household, or the most important part. Will you try me?"

"Like a suit? A car? A new barbecue?" Her voice squeaked. She gazed at him helplessly. "So important."

"Give me a run. Let me make love to you, let me tell you how much you and the children mean to me. I want to be your lover, their father. And I'll put my life on the line to prove it."

"You're offering me collateral?" Amusement slipped through the prudence, the waning ire.

He nodded vigorously. "Right. Since this is a very high stakes game we're in, I'll offer it up-front. My company and its assets, my majority stock in it, and its voting ability against your decision that I'd do a good lifetime job. Three months."

"You might lose your company." She was a fool. Nobody bartered a life—no, three lives— against a company. If she lost, she'd be bereft . . . and rich. Not really a good deal.

"I won't. But even if I did, you and the kids are worth ten companies. I can always start again, maybe do better. But I can't do better than you and the children for a family. I risk little, but I stand to gain a great deal. I'm a very innovative guy, and I can support you while you get your career revved up. I can also provide for the kids, make sure they get a first-class education."

"What a salesman you are," she said shakily. She swiped at her eyes, hesitating. "It's been spelled out what I get. What exactly is the deal for you?"

Rex stared at her for long moment. "The whole nine yards. A lifetime."

Words caught in her throat. She wanted to treat it lightly, pass it off. She couldn't.

"Three months. Is it too long?"

"No, but—"

"Fine, I can make it six months."

"No need—"

"Good. We have a deal. I think we should seal it with a kiss." He brought her out of the chair as he stood up. "Kiss me, beautiful lady. Please."

His soft, throbbing demand turned her to gelatin. Her hands rose as though they'd been ordered, clasping his face. She looked into his eyes. "I must be crazy," she muttered before placing her mouth over his. Jarred, alert with electricity, she could only sway in his arms.

"Delicious," he said against her mouth, parting her lips, letting his tongue blaze a trail to hers. Their twining, joining, became an erotic dance that spun them away from the room, from the house, from the county.

His hands lowered, clasping her hips, pulling her hard against his aroused body, grinding her sweetly against him, groaning his need.

"What are you doing?" Ira asked, suspiciously. "Does it hurt, Mommy?"

Louise was goggle-eyed, sucking her thumb industriously.

"No . . . thumb . . . Louise," Drew said, hanging on to Rex for fear of falling. "It . . . doesn't hurt, Ira," she told her son breathlessly.

"Oh. Rex is squeezing you."

Louise nodded, concurring with her brother.

Rex grinned, speaking around the jackhammer beat of his heart. "It doesn't hurt. It feels good. I like to kiss Drew. I want to do it all the time."

"Why?" Louise asked.

"Out of the mouths of babes," Drew muttered, trying to pull back from Rex and having little success. All at once she wondered why she had to be free of him. She was going to tell the truth . . . to the children and to herself. Slipping her arms around Rex's waist, she hugged his stiffened and surprised body. She felt his sharpened gaze but kept hers on the children. "Do you remember when I told you about your other mother and daddy?"

Louise nodded.

Ira nodded vigorously. "They went to heaven, but they still watch over us and love us, and they loved each other . . . a lot," he recited his catechism. "Now you're our mother, and you'll be it forever too."

Rex loosened his hold, more touched than he'd ever been, looking down at Drew. "That's wonderful."

"They were wonderful. And they loved each other totally. If they had to die, I'm glad it was together. They were gentle, smiling, laughing . . . and very good to each other and the world," Drew finished softly. "I'll always miss them."

"You told us that," Ira pointed out, practically.

"Yes, I did. Now, I'm telling you that I don't mind when Rex holds me and kisses me."

"Oh." Ira frowned, then nodded. "Okay."

"And there's one more thing." Drew inhaled shakily, burning her bridges. "Your other mama's daddy is coming to visit. He's your grandfather."

Ira frowned. "Is he going to live in our house? He'll have to take the room in the cupola. I've got my train set in the other bedroom. But he can come. We don't mind, do we, Louise?"

Louise shook her head.

Drew looked around at Rex. "I'm calling my lawyer. You should know that."

He nodded. "Good plan." He inhaled sharply, putting his forehead down on hers. "I want in, lady. Your life is important to me." He saw the palpable hesitation and was hurt, though he understood. "I'll keep knocking."

"You will?" Happiness welled in her. He wouldn't give up. She needed to know that.

"You know I will." He leaned down and kissed her again.

Ira frowned and looked at Louise. "He likes to do that. How do they breathe?"

Big-eyed, Louise shrugged, then followed her brother from the room.

Drew pulled back, breathless. "I . . . I still need time."

"You've got it," Rex said hoarsely.

The ball game was very exciting, even if Louise and Ira fell asleep halfway through.

When Drew looked at him hesitantly back in the hotel room, Rex touched her cheek with one finger. "You said you needed time, beautiful lady. I'll sleep on the couch."

They drove home in the van Rex had rented, comfortable, at ease, happy to listen to the childish chatter. They had a quiet day, and an early supper because the children were still tired.

Later in the evening, after the children were settled, Drew walked downstairs, out the front door, and down the steps. She crossed the lawn silvered by moonlight to the boathouse, then down the outside steps to the wide jetty. Stars winked like far-off flashlights in their summer constellations.

Rex was there, as she'd known he'd be. "Hi."

"Hi, yourself, Drew Laughlin." He moved slowly toward her, then pointed upward. "That's the Big Dipper, there's the Little Dipper . . . and Venus, star and goddess of love." He slipped his arm around her waist. "You're worried about seeing Justin."

"Yes." She inhaled shakily. "But I've made some decisions too. No matter what Justin decides, I won't give them up. They're mine." She paused, staring up at Cassiopeia, dwelling for a moment on the mother of Andromeda. Surely Greek mothers faced as many dilemmas as she.

"Tell me."

"I give you your three months," she said quietly.

Rex almost fell down. He was shocked, delighted, humbled . . . scared by all she'd handed him in six little words. "Oh, darling, you won't regret it." He tightened his grip, easing her back against him. "Are you swearing on the love star? Venus."

"Not just that one, but all of them. Summer skies in New York are wondrous," she said huskily.

"You're smiling. I can feel it in your middle," he said into her ear.

"I think I'm laughing at how bolluxed up my life is."

"Nah. It's simple, really. Go with it. It's just that we were a little like the traditional Fourth of July bash. Fireworks, explosions, great colors, flags waving." With each point he pressed kisses on her neck.

Involuntarily, Drew moved closer to him, pressing her hips into him, as though she'd always done so. When she heard his gasp, she closed her eyes and leaned fully on him. "Too late to back out now," she murmured.

"Don't want to," he said, his words slurred, as he moved his mouth over her hair. "I want to kiss you so much . . . but I have a feeling if I did, it could get out of control pretty fast."

Drew turned in his tight grasp, slowly, carefully freeing herself so she was inches from him when she faced him. "The three months start now, as of tonight. Right?"

Rex nodded. "But it's not going to start in the boathouse," he said huskily. He took hold of her waist and lifted her up, until her feet dangled above the earthen jetty. Their eyes and lips were on the same level. He smiled into hers. "My bed or yours?"

Drew laughed out loud, feeling exuberant. Sure, Justin would soon be at the house. There'd be questions, uncertainties, doubts. But she'd face them. And she fully intended to bolt, with the children, if it looked as though she was beyond her depth. Hopefully, it wouldn't come to that. "Mine—it's a double. Not big enough for you, but better than a single." She grimaced. "A bit shabby but clean—the canopy and bed, that is."

"I'll risk it." He bent slightly and swept her up into his arms, turning and striding up the steps and across the road to the yard.

He stumbled going up the porch steps.

"I'm heavy." She giggled into his neck.

"No. I'm anxious." He banged into the screen door and almost dumped both of them when he tried to open it. He cursed in a steady stream at his clumsiness and her growing amusement.

"I'll get it." Convulsed with merriment, she tried to grab the door. It banged twice. Three times.

"Shhh. You'll wake the children. And as much as I like them, I want to deal with you right now." He staggered and would've regained his balance if Drew hadn't laughed harder, hiccuping, her body arching as she tried to control herself.

Her movements rocked him. He tried for the door, staggered, hit his leg, the knee buckling. "Damn."

"Oops." Drew clung to him, caught in the certainty that she'd never had so much fun . . . and that she was going to land on her backside.

Down they went into the screen door, tearing the screen, bending the frame, sprawling in a tangle of arms and legs on the wraparound porch.

"I've . . . never . . . known such a romantic moment, ripping with sexual fire," Drew said, howling with laughter, clutching him.

"Quiet! They'll be down here in a minute." Rex was caught between frustration and hilarity. "My big moment. I blew it. Lord." He put his head in his hands, shaking it, leaning back against the doorframe. "And I'll damn well have to fix that screen in the morning." His grimace twisted upward in a sardonic smile. "Great, wasn't it?"

Getting to her knees, Drew leaned over him. "Did anyone ever tell you, you're a swashbuckler from hell?" Hilarity bubbled out of her. "I'm sure the neighbors have called nine-one-one." She put her hand over her mouth to stifle her laughter.

"Wonderful. What might've been the greatest night of my life I'll spend in jail?" Rex ran his finger down her cheek. "You're a beautiful hellion."

"Jail? Never!" Getting behind him, Drew put her hands under his arms, urging him up. "Heave-ho. Wow, you're heavy, Rex old boy."

"Thanks. I needed that." Scrambling to his feet, he glared down at her. "Don't think your Keystone Cops imitation has changed my mind."

"Or mine," she said softly, rising to her feet.

Dumbfounded, he stared at the hand she offered him. Clasping it, he pulled her closer. "You're the damnedest, sexiest woman I've ever known. But if you laugh again . . ." He saw the mirth in her eyes and groaned. "Did anyone ever tell you your timing is way off?"

"Uh-uh." She tightened her grip on his hand, tugging gently. "Let's go."

"I'll probably have a fatal accident before I get there," Rex said gloomily, trying not to smile at her renewed amusement.

"I'll help you up," she said softly, shushing him as they entered the house and crept up the stairs like partners in crime.

"So, this is what my friends mean when they talk about the lack of privacy once children are in the house."

Drew nodded.

When they entered her room and closed the door, the atmosphere changed, became charged; the humor dissipated. All the relaxed amusement they'd shared fled, leaving a surfeit of electricity.

"I've wanted you since the first day," Rex told her huskily.

"It took me a little longer. A few days." She tried to chuckle. She couldn't. "Strange. I never thought I'd feel attracted to a butler." She was babbling. She wanted him . . . but what if she couldn't let him love her? The old fear was in the back porch of her mind.

"Butlers are interesting," Rex told her, his

hands on her shoulder, stroking, edging the summer blouse off her shoulders. "They butle."

"I've heard that," she said throatily, wanting him mightily, not sure she'd have the strength to hold him.

He leaned down and touched her skin with his tongue. "Warm. Sweet."

"I'm . . . not . . . candy." Drew couldn't keep her eyes open. They drooped shut. "Very tough mother."

"Wrong." Rex let his hands slide to her waist, edging her closer, letting her feel his aroused body. "You're a bonbon I've wanted to taste for days."

"Things that happen too fast fade the same way." It couldn't happen to them. She needed him too much. The children loved him.

"Maybe. But sometimes when things are perfect, they don't need preliminaries, introductions, ordinary courtships. Our mating dance was done over children. Solid stuff. That's us. Not that I don't plan to court you. I think a long, slow preliminary can be very sexy, Andrew Laughlin." All the time he whispered, he disrobed her.

They hadn't turned on the light. Star and moonlight wafted in the room with the breeze, patterning the walls and ceiling in silver and gold, giving an argent sheen to the round area rug, making the walls and wood disappear in the glitter of their personal aura.

Rex threw off his own clothes, never taking his eyes from hers.

She held her breath, waiting for revulsion to assault her. Instead there was awe, wonder, want.

They stood close, not touching, nude, eyeing each other not quite clinically.

"I want you too," Drew mused. She shook her head. "Silly. Never thought I'd say that." She stared up at him, touching his chin with one languid finger. "I have something to tell you."

Rex saw the sudden trepidation. Though his body was racked with passionate need, he smiled gently. He brushed the hair back from her face. "Would you rather not make love?"

She looked up at him, a smile lighting her features. "No. I meant what I said. I want you." She led him to the bed with its mahogany footstool. "We have to climb up."

Rex stared at the canopied Victorian bed with its pineapple poles and crocheted top. "It's bigger than a regular bed."

Drew nodded. "Great-grandfather had the bed made in New York and brought up the Erie Canal. I've tried to bring back its luster with polish, but it could use refinishing." She was shaking with want, fearful of what he'd say, glad of the chance to tell him yet wondering if she should, knowing she must. She faced him, looking him over, liking what she saw. "I like your body, the way you're put together."

"Ditto," Rex said huskily.

"I'm aroused," she whispered.

"Ditto." His voice was a mere exhalation of air.

"But I want to tell you something. I went to boarding school in Wisconsin. My stepfather was in the diplomatic corps, and Mother traveled with him." She inhaled. "My first semester at Green Oaks, I was molested by a teacher."

"Damn," Rex drew out the word as though it could encompass the perpetrator.

Drew cleared her throat. "I was fourteen and cut off from family, as he well knew. I think it was mostly a control thing. Of course, I was so intimidated that I didn't say anything . . . at first. But it got worse. I instinctively knew he was approaching the time when there would be more than just . . . his hands on me." She gulped, tried to smile. "I blurted it out to my roommate one day. She called her father, a very important man in the community. The teacher was removed from the staff. I never saw him again. I was examined by doctors and psychologists. It was decided I should leave the school and be put into a fresh environment. My parents returned to the country." She stopped, looking down at their entwined hands. "Quite a brouhaha. I left the school . . . but maintained a secret friendship with my former roommate." She tried to smile. "You see, both sets of parents and the doctors thought it would be best if I severed all ties with the school."

"I can see how they thought that," Rex said calmly, struggling not to bellow his rage, break things, go after the damned crud who'd done it to her. "As I said, love, we can put this off to another time."

Drew shook her head. "Don't want that." She looked up at him. "I like being naked with you."

Her blinding smile and offhand remark didn't fool him. "There's more, isn't there?"

Drew nodded. "This shouldn't be so difficult to tell you." She shrugged. "I told you he put his hands on me. But I didn't tell you that I'm still a virgin." She swallowed. "I've never had an intimate relationship." But she wanted one with him. She needed Rex. Even more than that, she wanted him.

Stunned, Rex stared at her.

Silence stretched.

She looked away from him. "Hard to believe?"

"I'm grateful," Rex said quietly. "I wanted to kill him. I still do. But now I don't feel I have to go out and hunt him down this week. But the pond scum deserves being worked over for the physical and psychological damage he did."

Drew smiled. "Somehow I knew you wouldn't care."

"Oh, I care, a great deal. I care that anybody can be so darned callous with a child. I care that you would let me touch you. I care that you make me a gift of your virginity . . . though it wouldn't have meant diddly if you weren't one."

"I knew that too." Drew hitched closer. "I want this," she told him sadly. "Who knows? It could be my only chance."

In a flash of awareness he knew that there was more . . . and she wouldn't tell him. He opened his mouth to tell her he understood that, and shut it again. "I don't think so." He caught her close to him, his mouth worrying hers apart, his tongue entering, teasing hers.

Taking her with him, he fell back on the bed, the abrasion of skin rubbing skin sending his libido sky-high. He hitched backward, tugging her with him. "Don't want you to fall. You could break bones tumbling from this bed."

His slurred words fired her passion. He blotted out the sun of her pain, the moon of her memories. And she welcomed him, gladly. She parted her legs, bracing herself.

"Uh-uh. Sorry, darling. Not that quickly." Rex bent to her, chuckling in her ear. "We're both going to be pleading for it before I'm through."

"I want it already," she told him, surprised.

"You'll want it more." He curled her into his body, his hands and mouth moving over her, showing her how much he wanted her, stoking her fires with his desires. Her breasts were pressed to his, heaving upward with every tortured breath she took. He lifted his mouth, harsh surprise in his voice. "I don't need any more heat, yet you burn higher every moment." Holding her made him shake with desire. He wanted her with an elemental need that went beyond the sensual pull. He wanted her mind and spirit, the essence of her that made her the spirited person who'd adopted her friends' children, who'd fought to make a life for them, not only uncomplainingly, but joyously.

All of her made her sexy, not just the great body, the curvy, long legs, the dimples in her cheeks, the great skin that was a porcelain velvet. Her mind and soul melded her into the sensuous, desirable woman who had made all other women fade from his mind.

Rex sighed, his mouth moving down her neck, his teeth nipping at her skin. He loved the taste of her and wanted more. His hand slid up her passion-slicked body to cup her breast. Moving leisurely, loving the satiny feel of her, he opened his mouth over her, sucking there.

"Oh . . ." Drew's body arched, pulled by his passion and her own. Blood didn't flow, it cascaded, roared, blinded, deafened. She gripped his head, disappointed when he moved lower and left her moist breasts unattended. She would've laughed when he laved her navel, but she couldn't summon the strength.

Rex looked up. "I'm yours, darling. Please, remember that."

"I will." The words were a whisper in the argent room.

He pressed his face to her thighs.

When his tongue touched her most secret place, she arched and cried out, feeling she should protest but unable to as oceans of feeling swamping her, stealing her breath and words, robbing her of sanity, pillaging her good sense.

All of life became Rex. His hot, sweet mouth and hands captured her and kept her with him, loving him, wanting him. Love?

"Drew, darling," Rex crooned, feeling the flood build behind the dam of her heart, body, and mind. "Now, darling." He entered her in one sure stroke, and his being crashed in on him as she began to thrash and call out his name. He wanted to edge carefully past the barrier, but she wouldn't let him. She thrust against him, making him call out in the flood of excitement.

In a climactic apex of sensation, Drew had a sure knowledge that life would never be the same again.

Six

Justin was only a man. And he wouldn't remember. Over and over she said that to herself. But she'd not forget. Fear. Downright terror. Immobility. She owed him something, but she'd owed more to his daughter, her best friend . . . all those wonderful years when nothing could separate them.

Drew sighed.

"What's wrong, Mommy?"

She hadn't heard her son enter the room, Faulkner at his heels. She stared at him long and hard. He was nothing like her. Those brown eyes were his own father's. But he was hers. "A few glitches. But I'm working on it." That was true. She'd run afoul in her work. "Is everything all right with you?"

Ira nodded vigorously, smiling. "Rex said to tell you we have a visitor." The boy blinked when she shot off her high stool and stood in front of him flexing her hands. "What's wrong, Mommy? Are you mad?"

"Yes . . . no . . . surprised." She tried to smile. Surprised? Why? She knew he'd be there. Justin! "All right. I'll be right down." She looked down at her son. "Shouldn't you be in camp?"

Ira frowned. "Did you forget? Day off. Rex said we're on real vacation today, and we're going on boat rides and trips and things." He beamed.

"Did he?" She hadn't seen him that morning. He'd left her in the night, thinking she was asleep. She'd almost called him back, but perhaps it was better not to encourage the wonderful intimacy. He might be upset when he discovered what Justin could tell him. "Perhaps you and Louise would like to go over to—"

"We are," Ira interrupted cheerfully. "Mrs. Brewer is coming to get us."

Drew nodded woodenly. Nan Brewer was her next-door neighbor and a friend. She could bring the children back when it was time for Justin to meet them. The thought made her stomach flip-flop.

"Your tummy's burping, Mama," Ira said.

"So it is. Let's go, pal." She didn't touch him as she usually did. She didn't want him to feel her hand shaking.

She faltered in the hallway. The voices from the living room intensified her fear.

"'Bye, Mama. Mrs. Brewer's in the kitchen with Louise."

She waved at Ira, smiling sickly. She rushed over to give him a quick hug and kiss, ignoring his puzzlement. "Hurry. Don't keep Mrs. Brewer waiting. 'Bye." Watching until she heard the happy mix of voices fade from the kitchen, she crossed the hall, counted to ten, and entered the living room.

The two men turned toward her.

Drew didn't look at Rex. She studied Justin, seeing his preliminary puzzlement, the dawning recognition.

"You!" The shouted word from Justin, the way he jumped forward, had Rex moving in front of her, his eyes narrowing, his jaw tightening.

"What's going on?" Rex glanced from one to the other of the two tense people.

"Your name was Andrea Rutledge at Green Oaks," Justin said slowly.

Drew shook her head. "It was always Andrew. The registrar's office made a mistake that first year. I never corrected it."

"And the Rutledge?"

"That was my stepfather's name. I was very close to him, and to please him took his name. My own father died before I was school age. When it was time to take the children, I used my own, legal name," Drew said hurriedly, not looking at Rex.

"Drew?" he muttered, frustrated.

Justin looked at Rex blankly for a moment, then back at Drew as though he hadn't spoken. "You must've known that I loved my daughter."

Drew sighed, shaking her head. "I didn't doubt that. But you were a powerful man, used to having your own way. You showed, very openly, that you held David in contempt because he was an artist. That wounded Mary Justine deeply. I knew and she knew he was a wonderful person. You tried to change Mary Justine's mind. She was too much your daughter to put up with that." Drew swallowed. "She loved you, but she would never have let you come between her and David. They were two halves of a whole."

"And she loved you," Justin muttered.

Drew nodded. "From our first meeting we were sisters. We couldn't be separated. I'm still close to her," she said quietly.

Justin nodded, backing toward a chair and sinking into it. "I should have figured it was you and saved myself the trouble of hiring detectives to search for you."

"You might still have needed the detectives to find me. This is a *Laughlin* house."

Rex opened his mouth again, then thought better of it. He turned to a side table and splashed a small amount of homemade brandy into a glass. "Have some raspberry brandy, Justin. Drew's neighbor makes it. I sure as hell need something." He stared at Drew. When she nodded slowly, he gave her some, then tossed back the ruby liquid, wincing at the bite.

Justin paused as though he'd just crashed from a mountain into an unknown reality. He sipped the aromatic brew. "Potent," he remarked, his eyes never leaving Drew. "Would you believe I've regretted my every action toward Mary Justine and David? That I would do anything to make amends, though I can't." His lips trembled. "I didn't even get to say good-bye."

Drew went to the scarred oak desk and took out a rather yellowed letter she'd been keeping. "This is from her to you if you ever contacted me."

Justin took the paper, hands shaking. He leaned back in the frayed Victorian chair and began to read.

Drew glanced at Rex for the first time, her chin lifting when their eyes met.

"Explain."

She looked down at her hands. "It was my secret so long. I guess I felt I should talk to her father, but that I owed Mary Justine my silence. But now you know, anyway." She looked away from him. She felt unsure of him and herself. His face seemed to freeze over. Grief tore at her, but her eyes were dry. He hadn't understood her last night when she'd intimated it might be the only night of love she'd ever have. She had a doomsday surety she'd been right.

"Last night was important, Drew. You know that. So do I."

"Now is not the time."

Justin looked up at them, clutching the letter in his hand. "Rex came here because I begged him to see what sort of home my grandkids were living in, and not to let anyone know who he was. He didn't want to do it, Andrea—I mean Drew. The last thing he wanted to do was leave his business in the height of the season, but he did it for a friend." Justin folded the letter carefully and put it in his pocket, his eyes moist. "I had to know. Once I discovered their whereabouts . . ." He shrugged.

"The children are legally mine," Drew blurted.

"And you love them."

"Very much."

"The letter says as much, and that you'll be good to them, and that I'm not to try to take them away." Justin swallowed. "She forgives me, but wants the children with you because you have a good heart, and she wants them in an atmosphere of love."

Drew nodded. "She gave me much the same letter." She swiped at her eyes. "Believe me, I won't keep your grandchildren from you if you want to see them, but this is their home. They need to remain here."

Justin looked stunned. "You'd let me see them . . . visit them?"

Drew nodded. "But if you try to fight me for them, I'll fight back. They're legally mine."

Justin patted his pocket that held the letter. "So my daughter informed me." His smile was taut. "I've changed. After she died, I began to realize the need for compromise, that all life doesn't hinge on being the top man in a deal. Too late. I paid a damn big price to learn that. I don't want to be too late for my grandchildren."

"Why don't you stay for dinner and you can talk to them, tell them who you are. They know about you and your visit."

"Thank you," Justin said humbly, sitting back in his chair as though suddenly fatigued.

"Are you well?" Drew asked sharply.

Rex moved to his side. "I told you the trip could be too much."

"It wasn't. I've never felt better or been happier." Justin sighed. "I hope Mary Justine knows that. Maybe I'll rest on your wonderful wraparound porch this afternoon . . . after I've seen your restoration work, of course." He smiled up at Drew. "You're quite lucky, my dear, to have a man of Rex's ability doing your restoration."

Drew opened her mouth to tell the older man

she knew that, then she thought better of it. "It's quite cool out there."

Justin got to his feet. "Yes, I think I will use that lovely porch."

"Perhaps next time you visit, you'll stay with us," Drew offered tentatively.

He smiled ruefully. "I've already instructed my assistant to find a house to lease or buy in your neighborhood."

Drew grinned. "You think like your daughter."

"Thank you." Justin went out a floor-to-ceiling window, stepping carefully over the low sill.

Sighing, Drew faced Rex. "It was so simple. And I've feared it for so long."

"Why the hell didn't you tell me?" Rex demanded. Stabbed to the heart, he didn't reason that he'd come to her under false pretenses. He'd assumed she wouldn't hide anything from him . . . not after last night. Stupid. "Justin was the important man, the father of your roommate who contacted your family and arranged for the removal of your molester from the staff. Mary Justine remained your friend even though you were sent to another school."

Drew nodded. "We were always close, and we managed to get accepted to the same university, to room together again."

"You could've told me. Why did you hide it?" She shook her head. "It was buried so deep.

If Justin hadn't recognized me, I'm sure I would've told you, sooner or later."

"You could've trusted me."

She did trust him. "I guess I've put it on the back burner so long, it was hard to drag it out in the light."

"Last night was not insignificant," Rex said acerbically. "I thought that after such complete intimacy—" He broke off, his voice quavering.

Drew pulled back as though struck. She'd hurt Rex. And he was revealing it as openly, as emotionally, as a child. How could she make things right? Would he storm off?

"I've got things to do," he said tautly, brushing by her. "But I'm not packing," he told her without turning.

Relief almost made her drop to her knees. He wasn't going! Lord, she could have kissed the floor.

The meeting between the children and their grandfather went smoothly, largely because of Ira's guilelessness and persistence.

"You're the father of our other mother?"

"Yes," Justin said hoarsely.

"Then you can come at Christmas," Ira said happily. "We like Christmas, don't we, Louise?"

Louise grinned, nodding.

Justin looked taken aback, then joyous but uncertain.

"We would like you to come," Drew said quietly. "We need a grandfather, don't we?"

Ira and Louise nodded vigorously.

"Do we need a butler?" Ira asked, and frowned. "I like Rex. He's going to stay, isn't he, Mommy?"

Three adults stared at the children who smiled back at them.

"Yes . . . but we mustn't try to run other people's lives—" Drew began hesitantly.

"I'm staying," Rex said grimly. "Shall we eat? I made gumbo." He stared at Drew, then smiled down at the children. "You'll like it. It has sausage, shrimp, chicken, and rice, and lots of other good stuff."

"Your stint in New Orleans restoring several of those old buildings and redoing that brewery gave you a taste for Cajun cooking," Justin said, chuckling. "Drew, did you know that the city of New Orleans gave Rex a citation for the work he did?"

"Justin!" Rex said warningly.

"He doesn't like me to mention it, but we're all proud of him," the older man said, smiling impishly when Rex glowered. He took his seat at the table, staring out the open French windows to the porch. "I like this house, and the area. I think Rex's family will like it too."

Drew took her seat, smiling and nodding, happy that Justin was carrying the conversational ball. Rex was noncommunicative. "Yes. I like it. When I was a child—"

"What do you mean, my family will like the area?"

Rex's belligerent question brought salad forks to a halt. All eyes turned toward him. "Well, Justin?"

Justin looked up at Rex, smiling benignly. "It's been such a long time since you've seen your folks. Thought you might enjoy seeing them."

"Such a long time," Rex said sardonically. "I think I'm used to being separated from my family from time to time, Justin. What's up?"

Drew stared from one to the other, crumbling a roll on her plate.

"Tit for tat," Justin said softly, his eyes steady.

"And what the hell does that mean?" Rex asked.

"Just what I said. I owed you, dear boy. I thought I'd pay back a little."

"I pay back," Ira chimed in. "Mom says we have to if we borrow. Shall I call you Grandpa, or what?"

"Grandpa is fine," Justin said on a gulp, dabbing at his eyes with his napkin. "Sit down, Rex. I feel too good to spar with you."

Rex plunked down in his chair. "This isn't the end of it," he said brusquely.

"Are you mad, Rex?"

Rex fought a twisting inner battle, trying to smile at the boy and glare at Justin. "No. Just a little mixed up."

"Louise gets like that when she draws. I don't," Ira said complacently.

Louise smiled at Rex, nodding.

"What a sweetheart you are," Rex murmured, leaning over to kiss the top of Louise's head. "There's fruit, too, Ira. Have some grapes." Rex shoved the cheese and grapes to the grimacing boy. "If you want to play soccer, you have to eat fruit. Lots of vitamins."

Drew sat quietly, drinking it all in, wondering at her own placidity. Why wasn't it upsetting her? Justin had all but said that Rex's family would be arriving soon in the area. Clearly, he'd called them this afternoon. Why wasn't she running screaming into the night?

"Drew?" Rex offered the gumbo.

"No, thanks, I have plenty."

"You have none."

"Oh? Sure enough. All right, I'll have some." Justin must think she was crazy. He was smiling! About what?

Rex spooned gumbo into her soup dish. "Something's wrong," he whispered.

"That's getting to be normal around here," she whispered back.

Justin laughed. When Rex scowled at him, he buried it beneath a cough.

Instead of dawdling, as they sometimes did,

the children had single-mindedly worked their way through their food.

"I can have dessert. I ate everything. You can't, Mommy."

Ira leaned toward Justin. "Alonzo is our iguana. Wanna see him?"

"Yes," Justin said, surprised.

"Why doesn't everyone go out to the screened-in section of the porch, and I'll bring the ice cream," Rex offered hurriedly. "Alonzo can be out there with you for a while."

"Fine," Justin announced, his gaze going from Rex to Drew and back again, then down at Ira. "I think lizards are interesting."

"Me too," Ira said. "At first Mommy didn't want him, but now she likes him."

"I liked him . . . almost right away," Drew observed gently, smiling benignly on the departing group. "I'll help Rex with dessert."

"I want you to know I had nothing to do with inviting my family here. I was as surprised as you when Justin dropped his bomb." He ground his teeth, clenching his fists.

Drew looked at him calmly. "Your family sounds nice."

"They are," he said gloomily. "But I don't want them here. There are enough complications."

"I'm sure I'll like them."

He glanced at her sharply. "Something wrong with you?"

"Certainly not."

"Then why aren't you throwing things?" Rex stared at her glumly.

"Shall we join the others?"

"No." He rose to his feet, tossing his napkin at the table. It missed and fell to the floor. "I want it made clear that I'm not leaving, that I'm staying for however long it takes."

"You dropped your napkin." When he bent over to get it, she strolled out of the room.

"Don't think you'll . . ." Rex looked up. He was alone. What the hell was going on?

Seven

Three days passed euphorically for Drew, Ira, Louise, and Justin. They laughed, joked, talked, really getting to know each other. A relationship was building.

Rex sweated, fretted, and fumed. His life was slipping out of his grasp. He felt threatened and intimidated by Drew's placidity. His determination to stay hardened.

The next day the Dakeland family arrived en masse, noisy, excited, voluble, children and adults all talking at once.

Drew was entranced.

Rex was fuming.

"So, this is the little lady," Reuben Dakeland said, embracing a surprised but not displeased Drew. "Justin said you were a looker and that you'd knocked my son for a loop."

"Dad!" Rex glared at his family, red-faced.

"What an intriguing idea," Drew said sweetly. She glanced sideways at Rex. "Perhaps I should practice."

Under the hoots and laughter this engendered, Rex moved closer to Drew. "What the hell are you doing? I don't know you this way."

"Really? I rather like the new me. Try it, Dakeland. Just let go." Drew moved forward, speaking to Rex's sister from California.

Dumbfounded, he watched her move among his family, the children gravitating to his nieces and nephews. When Drew urged them to stay at the house rather than in the hotel, he stepped forward. "Now wait a minute—"

"Oh, that's right. I should ask the butler if the extra people would be too much," Drew said in dulcet tones, glancing at him, then looking back at his family.

"Butler?" The entire family chorused, grinning.

"I answered an ad," Rex said stiffly. "I'm sure Justin has filled you in, Maud."

His second sister grinned widely. "I love it. The big man is a butler. Drew, you must tell me everything. Maybe we should stay with you—"

"Never!" Rex glared at them when they laughed.

"But you'll all stay for lunch. We'll have a cookout," Drew announced.

"Just great," Rex muttered.

Louise moved next to him and curled her hand into his. "I wuv you," she said softly.

Struggling to hold back his emotion, eyes moist, Rex knelt in front of the child. "And I love you, beautiful girl."

Louise beamed and nodded. "I know."

Ira bellowed to her in his usual fashion, and she grinned, then wriggled free of Rex's hold to run from the house. "Coming, Ira."

Rex looked around the front room as though he saw it for the first time. Just let go. That's what she said. To hell with that. He was going to hold on with all his might. He stared out the window at the gathering of laughing, shouting people. His family. Chaos. Damn them. He smiled sourly. It was a damned conspiracy to keep him away from Drew. But he wasn't going to be thwarted.

Lunch was alfresco. If you could call the cacophony of laughter, games, eating, music, a picnic. It was wild and unruly, and Drew had never had such fun. Rex was run ragged. Her children reveled in the uninhibited affection and good nature of the Dakeland clan.

"Crazy, aren't they?" Rex said at her back.

She felt his hands at her waist. For a second only, she stiffened, then she leaned back, letting him take her weight.

"What is up, Andrew Laughlin?" he said against her hair.

She shook her head. "Nothing," she whispered back. "I told you, I just let go."

"And I'm supposed to know what that means? You've been fighting me, now you're not, is that it?"

She turned in his arms, her hands pressed against his chest. "Figure it out. Your family is fun. They want to try the waterskiing and sailing."

"What the hell—"

"Life's confusing," she said, chuckling, her fingers tapping his chest.

"You look happy."

"I am."

"I want you to always be that way."

"I think I will . . . all things being equal."

"What things?"

"Oh, the children being well, and growing strong. My work going well. And . . . other things."

"Spell it out."

"Figure it out."

"Damn you, Drew."

"Tut, tut, mustn't talk to the boss that way." Drew tapped him on the nose, laughing, moving away. It startled her when she was jerked back, banging against his chest, his mouth coming down like a brand on hers. She'd braced for violence. She got tenderness, a puzzled yearning. It struck such a fiery chord within her that for moments she didn't react, just held on and let the wash of sensuality take her.

He pulled her tight between his legs, wanting her to feel how she aroused him, how he wanted her.

She pulled back a fraction. "I want you too."

Shaken, he stared at her.

Drew lifted her hand to his face.

"Mommy, where's Rex?" Ira shouted from the doorway. They sprang apart. "There you are, Rex. You're on my team."

"What?" Rex looked at the child blankly.

Ira hit himself on the chest. "My team." He grimaced. "You've been kissing Mommy. It makes you dopey. C'mon." He turned and headed out the door again, yelling that Rex was coming after he had to kiss Mommy again.

"I think I'm going to have to put some tape on his mouth," Rex said thoughtfully, closing his eyes when he heard the shouts of laughter from various members of his family.

"You'd better kiss me first," Drew said, grinning.

"Yeah, you're right. But I'll be damned if I know what's going on in that head of yours."

"It'll come to you." She leaned against him, slanting her mouth across his, letting her tongue touch his, caress him, send her message clearly.

Rex groaned, deepening the kiss, wanting

her . . . loving her. "I damn well love you, Drew Laughlin." He pulled back, his hands on her shoulders, setting her back from him, and glaring at her.

"Thank you. I knew it'd come to you." She watched him stalk away, mumbling to himself, and chuckled. Justin had pulled her aside to sing Rex's praises. His words had merely confirmed what she knew intuitively about her man. He was everything she wanted.

That night when all were bedded down, most of the guests back at their respective hotels, Drew stood at her bedroom window, looking out at the lake. She was too caught up in the vortex of events to sleep.

Sighing, she went to her drawer, stripped down, and pulled on a diver's suit. Though she didn't relish swimming alone, knowing it could be dangerous, she wanted the wonderful solace that summer-night swimming could give.

Figuring there'd be less chance of waking the house if she went down the front staircase, she eased her way down and out the front door. Cap in hand, she walked across the yard and road, and down to the earthen jetty.

It was then she saw the other swimmer. She didn't need the silvery light of the moon to identify him. Rex! He was out quite a distance and was stroking furiously, as though to exorcise a demon.

Slipping into the water, she breaststroked quietly toward him, realizing he was so deep in concentration, he wouldn't notice her. His strong, sure movements carried him rapidly back and forth on a parallel line to the beach.

Taking a deep breath, she surface-dived quietly, barely rippling the water. Though it was dark, her goggles were clear, the moon like a beacon. She found him and moved up under him.

He jackknifed with surprise, taking them both down into the water. Rex surfaced holding her. "Couldn't sleep?" he gasped telegraphing that he'd had a workout.

"No." She hadn't intended to tell him, but with her new resolve wrapped round her like a cloak, she'd decided not to pretend about anything. "I wanted you in my bed."

"Damn! Marry me, Drew," he said roughly.

"When?"

"Now."

"Can't."

"Can." He bit gently on her lower lip. "I need you. And you know it."

"Yes, I do. Justin told me."

"Hell. I told you."

"I know. But I didn't believe you. I believed him."

He was treading water, holding her, staring at

her balefully. "Jeez, you know how to hurt a guy."

"Let's swim first." Drew stroked lazily out into deeper water, following the cone-shaped strip of moonlight on the water, sighing with contentment over the silky abrasion of fresh water on her skin.

Rex stayed with her, admiring her graceful, almost effortless movements. When she turned on her back, he did the same, and they stroked toward shore. Drew had changed, curved out, blossomed. He didn't know how or why. It alarmed and titillated him, intrigued and irked him. Damn her! She knew he loved her. His agitation made him flail his arms, take in water.

"Take it easy. I have you. Cramp? Don't worry, we're in shallow water." Drew grinned comfortingly at him.

"I'm all right. And stop that."

"What?" Her grin widened.

"That." Swiping at the droplets on his face, he stood in the waist-high water.

"I'm smiling," she said gently.

"I know," he said. "I just don't know why."

"I'm happy," she said simply. "I let go."

Rex stood close to her, his mouth opening, closing, opening, closing. "And I damn well will never let go."

She reached up and touched his face with one finger. "Aww, go ahead. Let go."

When she climbed up the jetty ladder, he

watched the graceful sway of that slender body
and shook his head. She'd turned into a mys-
tery woman with a Mona Lisa smile. She had
him on a string, and she was tugging. Did she
know he'd go willingly? Let go? He wanted to let
go of everything but Drew Laughlin and her
children.

She turned when she reached for her towel.
"Want to share?"

"I have one," he said huskily. "I want to
explain about my family."

She shook her head. "Don't. I like them. And
it's good for the children . . . and Justin to
have them here. New relationships are important."

"You don't resent Justin's presence, or that
he's planning to buy a home in the area?"

She shook her head. "I thought I would. No, I
was fearful of him, and that made me resent-
ful . . . but he doesn't want to part the children from me . . . and I can share them." She
sighed. "They need a grandfather." She slung
the towel over her shoulder and started up the
incline to the road.

He moved next to her, reaching out impul-
sively to take her hand when a driver hurtled
past them on the narrow lake road. "Damn
fool," Rex muttered, his arm bent through her
arm, to keep her close to his side.

Drew looked up at his scowling face, and
laughed.

He looked down at her, his smile hesitant. "What's so funny?"

"You. Your jaw's out a mile, and you look like you could bite through steel." His smile twisted sensually, and her heart accelerated.

He leaned down slowly, his mouth moving toward hers, hesitantly, as though he'd give her ample time to refuse him.

Impatiently, Drew reached up and cupped his strong jaw with both hands, bringing his mouth to hers. As they touched, she spoke. "Don't you think I've waited long enough?"

Rex groaned. "The house is filled to overflowing with my family. Some won't be in their own places until late tomorrow." He bent over her, placing his mouth gently on hers, taking more, his heart thundering when her lips parted.

Drew pulled back from the long, drugging kiss, her eyes sleepily gazing at him.

Another car whizzed by.

"Well, we can't stay here. Come along, butler, I'll show you something that you haven't cleaned." She took his hand, leading him along the road.

"Your office?" Then he paused and frowned when she turned toward the wooden bridge that led to the upper floor of the boathouse.

"This is my getaway. Sometimes I bring the children here, but mostly I come by myself."

Rex stared at this room. He'd used the phone

on the ground floor to call Justin. He'd never been up here. The room was large. Cathedral ceiling. He'd have to duck if he walked too close to the walls. Two dormers looked out on the lake; one on the south side gave a panoramic view down the east side of the lake. A thick rug of rich alpaca dominated the wood floors with huge pillows in hues of orange, coral, and peach strewn about. No television. One swing lamp for reading. Silence. "It's wonderful. Why haven't you let me clean it?"

Drew shrugged. "Just habit, I guess. I come down once a week and go over it, and it's here for me when I need it." She opened the east windows and let in the lake breeze, then turned and sank down on the alpaca rug, yoga fashion. "So you like my hideout."

"Very much." He settled down in front of her. "Privacy. What we need."

"Why?"

Startled, Rex gazed at her. "What did you say?"

"Why do we need privacy?" She grinned.

"You know why," he said, eyes narrowing on her. She was doing it again. Disappearing on him. She was as elusive as a soft leaf, floating on the breeze . . . yet there was a tangible determination to her he'd not seen earlier. "I want to make love to you. What do you want?"

"With what in mind?"

"Hell, Drew, this isn't a game I'm playing."

"Good, I'm not into games, either. As sexy as I might feel, I can't forget I'm a responsible parent."

"Are you sexy?"

"Yes. Did you hear the rest of what I said?"

"Yes. I'm damn sexy myself."

"It works better that way," she said softly, then giggled.

Rex shook his head, leaning toward her and taking her hand. "This demands candlelight and wine."

"This demands two committed people," Drew retorted.

"We have that."

"So we do."

Rex stretched out on the floor, tugging at her hand so that she curled next to him. "I want you, badly. I need you just as much," he said huskily. "But I have to ask what you mean by letting go."

Drew leaned over him, letting her hair curtain him. "I was sure you'd know." She looked up at the ceiling, sighing. "It was Justin—not just his arrival, his vulnerability, that he had the same fears I had of loss. It was his deep perception of things that had him telling me about you."

"Lord," Rex groaned, bringing her hand to his mouth. "He's treated me like a son, not a godchild. I could always go to him with any problem, and he could generally come up with a path to take if not a solution. But he does carry on—"

Drew shook her head, letting her hand press down on his mouth again. "He told me that you're loving . . . and giving . . . and willing to help out." She looked down at him.

It shocked Rex to see the silvery sheen of tears on her cheeks. "Drew?"

"I'm being silly. But don't you see, I was holding back, drawing in, keeping myself protected from . . . What? You? How foolish. I knew what you were. It isn't easy to have children in the house. They swell up, take up living space, absorb the oxygen, the energy, the time, and any inclination to do anything more than care for them. I knew that, and I saw you tackle it . . . and overcome it."

"I love them, Drew," Rex said slowly, not sure he comprehended her meaning.

She nodded vigorously. "Oh, I've never doubted that. Not since Ira's friend got chocolate ice cream on your beautiful trousers. Each day I saw you do things that were alien to you. I've kept house for those two long enough to know when someone's in virgin territory—"

"How you talk," Rex murmured, his smile slipping when she grinned at him.

"Roué." She leaned down and kissed his nose. "You know what I mean. The day the dishwasher backfired—"

"Too much soap. I was a fool not to look at the directions on the box."

"Don't interrupt," she admonished him, running an inquiring finger over his neck and chest, smiling when he caught his breath. "I'm extolling your housewifely virtues. They'll all add up to a fine résumé."

"Do I need one?" Rex whispered.

"Oh, I think so."

Her throaty answer, and her eyelashes drooping sensuously over her glittering eyes, had his heart hammering up into his throat, his blood cascading through his veins. "I might faint," he told her roughly, "if this is halfway to what I think it is, it'll be too much for me."

"We've just begun. Don't rush it." Her hand scored over his chest as she leaned down and kissed one masculine nipple.

"I won't," he managed to say hoarsely. "I hope my medical insurance covers this type of heart failure."

"It will. Or I'll go halves with you on the bill."

"Kind of you."

"So, getting back to Justin and his talk, I began to realize that you'd be a great catch for a mother with children."

"Thank you."

"Outstanding, in fact. So I let go."

"Wise of you," Rex said, hyperventilating.

"Yes, I thought so. I let my inhibitions go and

decided on a positive plan of attack with a hopeful result."

"Which is?" Rex's lips were so dry, he could barely form the words.

"That you and I should come together, archaically speaking. And I think we can live together. We've actually done that."

"Yes, we have." Roaring blood was driving his pulse rate sky-high. He'd never been more hopeful, or happier. "Go on."

"But in order for us to really live together, we needed to find out if we're sexually compatible."

"You're laughing, damn you. And you know we are. And I'm as aroused as hell by what you're saying."

"So am I." She leaned over again, chuckling when his hands came up and held hers.

"Stretch out your legs," he murmured.

"All right." In two lithe movements she was on her stomach next to him, gazing into his eyes, just centimeters from her own. "You have gorgeous, very sexy eyes, Rex Dakeland."

"Umm, so do you." He touched her chin with one finger, bringing her close to him, his lips rubbing against hers. He grinned ruefully. "I'm nervous, and it's not our first time."

"I'm confident," she said softly.

"I've never been in love. It's different."

"Very."

"I like it." Rex lifted her as though she were a

feather, and placed her the length of his body. "I like you here."

His rough voice almost unbalanced the control she'd kept on her rampaging emotions. "I want you, Dakeland."

"You're going to get me."

"There's one more thing you should know, Dakeland."

"We're off first names and onto last?"

"At this point we are."

"Okay, Laughlin. Shoot." His hardening body was a sweet pain. He'd never experienced such throbbing need.

"Okay. I want the whole ball of wax, big guy." She grinned at him.

Rex nodded. "So do I."

She giggled. "Good." She wriggled on top of him to get comfortable.

"Don't!" Rex gasped, fighting for control. "It'll be over before it's started."

"Oh. Sorry. Just getting comfortable. Is that better?"

"No, but go on," he said between his teeth.

"Nothing more, really. I just needed to set the record straight." She looked thoughtful. "It's amazing how hot you made me the first time."

"Thank you . . . I think." Rex groaned. Her body sent lightning streaks through him. He was burning from the inside out. He'd explode with it. Nothing had ever been so torrid.

"Are you listening to me?"

"Trying my damnedest, believe me. You're arousing as hell." He tried to smile at her when she laughed, but it was a poor effort. It took all his concentration to listen to her.

"Whatta team." She scored a finger down his chest. "Rah. Rah."

"Yeah." He gulped.

"A mama who was a virgin. Do I qualify for the record book?"

"No, but I may. As the man who was too excited to make love to the woman he was on fire for," Rex said huskily.

"Fear not, I'll get you started." She kissed his ear, nibbling there, then let her mouth move down that strong neck, those wonderful muscles bulging with strain. "Are you glad or sad that we've settled things?"

"Glad," Rex muttered, his mouth roving over her neck.

"You don't think I'm frigid for waiting so long?"

Rex opened one eye. "You're miles from frigid, lady. And if I didn't love the position I'm in, I'd get up and dance a jig that I was your first."

"Good. I'm happy about that too."

The other eye opened. "And all things being equal, I'd like to be your last, as you'll be mine. At least I'd like you to ponder that idea." His hands went over her, as though each pore was too special to miss. "I want to be your one and only, Drew Laughlin."

"Sounds very appealing, especially now." She'd tried to keep it light, but his touch had made her eyelids turn to lead, her body to jelly. Yet inside she was churning with a growing passion that awed her. "I never thought there could be such emotion," she said, her voice breaking.

"I feel the same," he murmured. "God, you're wonderful." Her mouth had moved over his face, exploring, sucking, kissing. She was a wanton voluptuary . . . and she was his. He expanded with joy.

"I really like this," Drew said, surprised happiness bubbling from her. "Making love is really fun."

"If you can hang on," Rex said through his teeth as she moved against him.

"Relax, big boy. I'm going to make you feel good."

"Oh, I know that. I'm well on the way." Rex closed his eyes, his hands flexing on her soft body, his fingers working the straps of her suit down her arms.

"Umm. I love your chest. Broad. I like the way the hair curls, just a bit." She pulled and tugged gently there.

"Right." Breathing was not working. He could barely get enough air. He had to go slow. Savor the delight. It had to be right. His hands went over the smooth curve of her buttocks, and he moaned.

"Be strong. Drew to the rescue."

"Rescue, hell. You're killing me."

Drew laughed shakily, feeling very much pulled apart herself. "Are you telling me I'm doing it wrong?"

"I'm telling you you're very, very right." He clasped her around the middle and put her to one side.

"Oh. I thought you would—"

"Shh, love, it's coming. I want you to be ready. And you will be, sweetheart." He leaned over her, kissing her slowly, gently, completely. His mouth was hot, hungry, taking and giving, firing her as he did himself.

Drew couldn't hold back. He'd pulled her into the vortex, and she was wild, unfettered, spun into the satin trap of sexual love. It all came back in a blinding flash, all the emotion and passion she felt the first time seemed to mushroom around her, grow hotter, expand more beautifully. It was even better, because now she was not just a wanting participant, she was a knowledgeable one. She felt caught by him, fluttering upward eagerly to meet his demanding passion, even as her own passion wove its web around him. Nothing had prepared her for the heat, the desire, the first time. And now, when she knew, it still made her quake from head to toe. When he shook with desire, she trembled in his arms.

His mouth moved slowly to her neck, savoring

the hot, smooth skin. His tongue invaded her ear, beginning the rhythm that his body longed to imitate. When she whimpered her pleasure, the erotic sound sent his libido soaring.

Her breasts were beautiful! He hadn't forgotten. They'd been in his dreams, day and night. Soft but firm, uptilted, teasing, the pink nipples demanding his attention. In loving concentration he took one into his mouth, worrying it with teeth and tongue until it pouted into hardness.

"Rex!"

He lifted his head, smiling sleepily. "Yes, love, I know." He bent over her other breast, loving it the same way. Then he moved lower, his tongue circling her navel.

"Rex?"

"Shh, love, it's right. I want you to be ready. You will be."

"Oh." Drew didn't know what to expect. His lovemaking was all new to her, but she could recall every gentle stroke with delicious clarity. She was soporific and more alert than she'd ever been. The paradox was enervating . . . and energizing. When his tongue circled her navel, she arched, gasping, unable to comprehend how his mouth could set her skin aflame with want, almost as though it had parted from the flesh and had a pulsating, writhing life of its own. "Nooo," she said more in reaction than response as his mouth moved lower and she knew what he would do.

Rex lifted his head. "Don't you want me, darling?"

"No . . . yes . . . I didn't think . . ." Drew's hand flailed for a moment, then settled on his head. "Yes," she said softly. His lopsided grin made her heart flip over. "Very much." She smiled at him. "I'm all at sea."

Rex moved lower, gently lifting her hips.

When his tongue intruded, Drew cried out, feeling a hot rush of feeling so wonderful . . . so alien . . . she could only cry out his name.

"Go with it, darling, go with it, I'm with you." Rex moved up her body, pushing between her legs and into the warm, moist cavity. Only a gentle thrust took him through, but she felt virginal to him, and he took every care. Then he was fully inside her, possessing her as she possessed him.

"Rex!"

Her scream was covered by his mouth as he began to thrust. When she thrust back, he knew he couldn't hold on. He'd never been so hot. "I want you, Andrew Laughlin," he said desperately.

In ardent communion they took each other, exploding in feeling in the age-old commitment that only true lovers know.

Silence. Long moments passed. Hands moved indolently over skin. Sometimes they touched and clung, fingers entwining. Words were only exhalations.

Drew opened her eyes, glancing at him, biting her lip. "It's quite something, isn't it?"

"It is." He brought her hand up to his mouth, kissing each finger. "As long as you know this changes things, Drew." He eyed her steadily, noted the trepidation, the hesitation, the questions. "Some people go a lifetime and never imagine what we just had, let alone experience it. And we had it our first time too. I won't throw it away. And I won't let you throw it away."

Eight

Drew opened her eyes and began worrying. She knew at once she was still in the boat-house . . . and alone. She sat up, her hand going to her mouth, rubbing her swollen lips, her body beginning to tingle as though it, too, recalled last night.

The world had changed. She'd found out many things in the throes of love, their first night together and last night. Passion was a shared commodity, not something that belonged to man alone or woman alone. Most important, she'd discovered a capacity for sexual love that she hadn't guessed at. She'd always known she could love deeply—she'd already found that depth measureless when it came to her children. She hadn't realized that she could give all her love to a man, and once giving him the love, regiving it, over and over again.

She sneaked into her room through the fire escape. Rushing through a shampoo and shower, she hurriedly dried her hair, brushed it off her face, and twisted it to a circle on her neck. She donned fresh cotton slacks in taupe with a deep orange cotton blouse and brown sandals. She had a great deal of work to do, but first she'd see to the guests.

Assuming that Rex had made breakfast—no doubt they had all begun eating—she went right to the great room. She paused when she heard Ira's high voice.

". . . and that's going to make us happy. Right, Rex?"

"You bet."

Puzzled, Drew strolled into the room, then stopped. They were all there. She smiled tentatively at a beaming Justin. "Good morning."

Justin rose to his feet, his arms outstretched. "My dear, I'm so happy for you. And I couldn't be more pleased."

Drew tried to smile when he embraced her.

When the rest of the family stood behind him, taking their turns at hugging her, she glanced sharply at Rex. He smiled benignly. Something was up! She leaned closer to him, her crocodile smile straining her mouth. "What's going on?"

Rex laughed, drawing Ira's attention. "Your

mother wants to know what's going on," he said. "Isn't that funny?"

Ira guffawed, bringing smiles to the faces of Rex's family. "You make me laugh, Mommy, when you pretend you don't know. Louise and I are glad."

"Are you?" Drew whispered, her smile fluttering from one to the other of Rex's relatives. "Then I'm glad too."

Ira laughed louder. Louise grinned. The guests chuckled.

Drew glanced at Rex, narrow-eyed.

He put his arm around her. "Darling, I know I should've waited for you, but the children were so excited, I let them announce it."

His grin was fatuous, stupid . . . out of character. It set her teeth on edge. There was something feral, deadly, about it . . . determined, set on course with no turning back. "How sweet. Now you can tell me."

"All right," Rex said dulcetly, leaning down to kiss her ear. "The enamel on your teeth will disappear if you continue to grind them that way."

"Tell me . . . please."

Ira grabbed her hand. "Rex told everybody he's going to be our daddy." Ira looked thoughtful. "He told us first when we were having our oatmeal, didn't he, Louise?"

Drew reeled, watching the little girl nod shyly

through a hot mist of surprise. "Did he? I'm not sure I know."

"Sure, you do. We're going to be married. I let the children announce it."

Silence.

"Maud, please take the children outside . . . all of them," Rex said.

Drew reddened.

Rex stood, glaring at his family as his sisters shepherded the children from the room. He glanced quickly at Drew. "Calm down."

Drew tittered, then giggled, then started to laugh.

Rex grabbed her arm, pulling her to her feet. "We'll talk in your office. "

Once there, he said, "Listen to me."

"I am." Fantasyland. That's what this was. Drew felt she was having one of those life-like dreams that made you positive you'd lived it.

"Dammit, Drew, don't slip away from me."

"I'm not. But you'll have to admit this is insane. You shouldn't have told the children we'd marry, not when we hadn't discussed it." It was wild, wonderful. Unreal. She couldn't allow her emotions to get so unchained, to float toward the clouds. She was a mother, a responsible citizen, a homeowner . . . tax-payer.

"Will you marry me?" It was so damned important, it turned him to soft wax to verbalize what he'd been saying in his mind for days.

"Now you're asking me?"

"Begging is a better word. Don't turn me down, Drew. Everything between us has been backward since we met, turned around, upside down. And this morning when I looked at you lying next to me in the boathouse, I knew it had to be that way, forever."

She stared at him. "Upside down?"

"You know what I mean. And don't laugh. Package deal. And I won't give up on you or the children—"

"Glad to hear it."

Rex grinned lopsidedly. "I want you. But I want them just as badly to be my children. My mother said that Louise has my eyes."

Drew bit her lip, caught between laughter and tears. "She does? I thought she looked like me."

"Nah. They both look like me."

Her amusement faded. "It's a tough world . . . painful sometimes. We could lose. A great many good people do."

"We won't."

"Wisconsin is far away."

Rex shook his head. "The moon is far away. Wisconsin and New York are only a step apart. I do renovating downstate."

"Schools?"

"We have them in Wisconsin."

She nodded dumbly.

"You want them to remain here," he said softly.

"They need stability, not another upheaval." Fearful, hovering on the brink of pain and ecstasy, she watched him.

Rex nodded slowly. "All right. We locate here and keep the farm in Wisconsin for when we visit at holiday time." He saw the tears form and spill over. "Don't cry, love," he said huskily.

"Got to."

"Nah. Let's celebrate. Tell my family we'll marry, and do it. Then we'll go on a honeymoon with our kids."

"A honeymoon with kids? Wow. What an innovative idea."

"I thought you might like that."

Drew walked over to her desk, pulling and pushing at the pens clustered in the well. "Think we can pull it off?"

"I know we can." He shrugged. "We have to succeed. It's all I have."

The simple declaration had her trembling. "It's like falling off a mountain. One minute you're at the top. The next second you're plummeting, end over teakettle, out of control." She shook her head. "Scary."

"Not if we're together."

Her smile was fleeting. "There's that."

"Always that."

"Tell me how Ira and Louise reacted this morning."

"Well, I fortified my arguments with oatmeal . . . and brown sugar."

"Serious offensive weapons."

"I thought so. Then I plied them with fresh-squeezed orange juice, all the while extolling my many virtues."

"All two?"

"Brat. I have more than that. Three."

"My mistake."

Rex pulled her into his arms and kissed her deeply. "Then they told me that it'd be a good idea if I stayed with them and you. I damn near cried."

"Don't be silly," Drew gulped, tears raining down her face.

Drew couldn't comprehend the happiness. It was too deep, too high, too wide and warm.

"Has my mother or father made you uncomfortable?" Rex asked later that day.

"No, no. I like your mother . . . your family."

"Good. Do you like me too?"

The ingenuous question coming from the hard-bitten, self-made man rocked her. "Yes, yes, I like you." "Love" was the operative word, wasn't it?

"That's a start." Rex felt as though he'd geared for battle. "It's important that we see eye-to-eye," he said hesitantly. "Good for the children."

"Stable environment."

"Right. You've made them happy. I want it to stay that way."

"Can't fight a lot."

"Hell, no."

"Keep everything smooth."

"As silk."

"But talk things out."

"Everything."

They stared at each other for long moments.

"We sound like we're cementing a business deal," he said carefully.

"Well, I suppose we are."

"Yeah, well, I want that . . . but I want you, too, naked, needy, and mine."

His blunt declaration had her gasping. "Cut right to the chase, don't you, Dakeland?"

"Yes, ma'am. Are we back to last names again?"

"Somehow it seems safer," Drew muttered.

Rex touched her arm. "Did I hurt you last night?"

Drew shook her head, without looking at him.

"I loved it. You were so beautiful."

As though her head were on a rubber band, it snapped his way. "You were beautiful too." She watched the blood chug up his neck. "Have I embarrassed you?"

"No! You've made me happier than I've ever

been. And your saying what you did is the icing
on the cake. Could we begin making long-range
plans? I'll give you all the credentials you ask
for. I've a degree from Wisconsin. I wasn't stupid. I also played sports, so I can help Ira when
he's on teams. You know I'm good around the
house—"

"Whoa. Once you get started . . ." She shook
her head.

"Don't interrupt. I don't want to forget anything. I haven't baked much since I've been
here, but I can. I make a blueberry kuchen
that'd knock you out. I can even sew. Nothing
fancy and I've never tried needlepoint or things
like that, but I bet I could do them. "

"A true Renaissance man."

"Try me."

"I did, last night. I liked it."

"Try me for the long haul," Rex said huskily.

"I'm giving it serious thought."

"You'd better, since our forthcoming marriage
was announced."

"That's right."

Rex nodded his head slowly. "And nothing
will interfere with that."

"It seemed unreal at first, not now."

"I told my family they might as well hang out
until the ceremony—"

"What? You expect them to . . . you think
that I . . . how can you even imagine . . .
why that'd be weeks—"

"Will you finish what you're saying before you hop on something else?"

"Don't you interrupt me, you . . . you . . ."

They glared at each other, so intent that they didn't hear the door open again or see the woebegone face staring at them.

In the sudden silence they heard the sob and whirled toward the door.

"Oh, Louise . . . darling . . ."

"Louise, sweetheart."

Rex and Drew spoke at the same time.

Louise looked from one to the other, then spun around, bolting from the room.

"Now look what you've done," Rex accused.

"Me?"

They both rushed to the door, getting caught in the doorway.

"Me first. I'm her mother."

Drew shot ahead of Rex, scowling at him.

"Hurry up, she was crying," he said accusingly.

"I know that."

They catapulted out of the house onto the porch, into an assembly of frowning Dakelands, spouses, and children.

"It only needed this," Rex muttered.

Louise was cuddled on Justin's lap crying into his shoulder, wailing unintelligible phrases into his ear while her hot tears coursed down his neck.

"She says you don't love her, Mommy, and you don't want her to have a daddy," Ira said in tones that would've done credit to a Pavarotti, booming as they did over his enrapt audience. "She said she wants a daddy," Ira said dolefully. "Sad," he finished.

"Ira," Drew said warningly, recognizing her son's dramatic intonations. That Ira was a con-summate entertainer was no news to her; that he knew he couldn't fool her but might sway a stranger was something both mother and son knew.

"Don't scold the boy, dear," Winifred said gently, gathering him to her. "He's upset."

"He will be," Drew said under her breath, as her son turned his head and looked up at her expectantly.

Ira let out a wail that had all the Dakelands bending toward him and alternately glaring at Rex.

"Ira!" his mother said again.

"I'm . . . I'm all right," he said pathetically.

"You and I should have a talk and—"

Louise wailed from her sanctuary on Justin's lap.

"I don't know how you can smile at this, Son, but I tell you now, I don't approve," his father said, patting ineffectually at Louise's head. "This is not nurturing the way we knew it," he said frostily, glaring at his eldest, his glance filled with disappointment when it touched Drew.

"Sir," she began, meaning to fully explain her son's childlike attempts at manipulation.

"Right, Dad," Rex interrupted winningly, gazing down at Ira, who looked back. He understood his son-to-be very well. "I don't intend to deny these two a father. I make a solemn promise in front of all these people that I'll marry their mother—"

"Rex!" Surely he'd wait for a more opportune time.

". . . as soon as possible. Today's Tuesday. We'll set it up for Saturday. Can we do it, Justin?"

"I know a few people in New York, more than a few." Justin all but jumped from his chair, settling Louise into Maud's willing arms. He rubbed his hands together, looking thoughtful. "Yes, yes, I do know people who'll get this moving for us. Action, that's what we need." He grinned at Rex and Reuben. Then he reached for Louise again. "I want my grandchildren in capable hands. I'll get on it. Come along, my sweet thing, you come with Grandpa and we'll make some phone calls. Winifred, you're in charge of getting the right clothes for everybody. Call Bendel's in Manhattan. That should get things started. Reuben, you call those caterers who do such a fine job in Milwaukee. If they can't handle it, tell them to give you a name in Manhattan, or this area. . . ."

Words streamed out behind him, and he was gone.

"But . . . but . . . wait a minute." Drew tried to stem the flood of Dakelands heading off the wraparound porch, eyes glittering with intent.

"Never mind, Drew, we'll handle it," Maud said, beaming. "Monica, go with Daddy and take notes when he touches base with the caterers; otherwise, he'll forget something. For heaven's sake, no ice swans, if you please. So tacky. I'll help Mama with the flowers and music. . . . You children play nice with your cousins now. They've had a shock today." She threw kisses at Ira. "Of course your mommy loves you. And you're getting a daddy. Play a game, and we'll go shopping this afternoon." She frowned at her sister. "Maybe we should fly into New York."

"New York?" Drew was stunned.

Monica frowned at her. "Are you getting a headache? Don't worry. Let's go, everyone. Quickly. This will be so nice if we all do our jobs." She put her hand to her mouth. "The church! Most important." She pointed at Drew. "You call. You'll be happier in your own church."

In minutes, Rex and Drew were the only two on the porch.

Drew stared at him, stunned and dry-mouthed. "You set that up."

Rex shook his head. "Didn't have to. Our wise children did it."

"This can't be happening." Her knees had melted, her stomach was doing handsprings . . . and she was getting a heck of a pain behind her eyes.

"It is."

"Farcical."

"You're the one who said to let go. I did. Now you're wheezing. Do you suffer from asthma?"

"Not yet." She could barely make a fist. She should hit him, but he was right. She'd been the one who'd gotten uptight, and after promising herself she'd let go. Let go! A rosy picture was interfering with her determination to fight Rex, to stand independent of him. Married to him! Incredible! Crazy! "It couldn't work," she mumbled.

Rex put his arm around her. "Why?" It annoyed him more than he liked to admit when she said that, but it didn't put a damper on his intent to woo and win her. "Children need a father. Right?"

"Yes, but—"

"Wait, let's take it one step at a time." He led her off the porch, ambling toward the water.

"Where are we going? Not the boathouse . . ." Liquid fire lapped at her when she recalled those precious moments. "Cool heads," she whispered hoarsely.

"We'll be cool. In fact, we won't make love until we're married. How's that?"

"Fine," Drew said dazedly. Then, realizing what she said, she dug in her heels. "We're getting married."

Rex nodded slowly. "I think we are. My family loves a party."

"That's not a good enough reason to wed," she said faintly.

"It's better than some people have." He took her arm, leading her away from the house. "We should look at the pluses, for a change, and leave the minuses. . . ."

"We should." Weak as a kitten, riddled with hope, she let him lead her down the curving stone path to the road. On the other side was the lake . . . and the boathouse. "What if we don't get along?" she mumbled.

Rex bent over her, laughing. "We will. We already do."

"Not all the time."

"No one gets along well all the time, unless they're made out of wax." Her pitiful attempt at a smile had him chuckling harder. "You're looking for bogeys again."

"I can't help it. I'm a mother. I'm allowed to be a pessimist," she said gloomily.

"You can look at the bright side too," Rex said gently, leading her into the boathouse.

"I shouldn't be here. I have a lot to do."

"To prepare for our wedding?"

"Yes. No!" She rolled her eyes at him. "To make a living."

He opened the door, let her precede him, followed her, then gathered her into his arms. "Let's give it a chance."

She looked up at him, enjoying being held by him, feeling safe.

When she grinned, he blinked at the sudden change. "What now?"

"The butler did it," she said, chuckling. "That's been going through my mind for two days."

Rex put his forehead down on hers. "Is that a yes?"

She leaned back, looking up at him. "How much do you want this?"

"A whole lot. How about you?"

"I don't want to want it that much."

"How much?"

"A good deal," she said cautiously. "But . . . but I know that marriages are now a throwaway commodity. And I'm a great believer in saving, in ecology. I don't like to throw away."

"Neither do I. So let's make a pact. We don't throw away."

"Divorce is common."

"We'll make it obsolete."

Drew reached up and touched his cheek, her

smile fleeting. "It isn't just our decision to make or break this. I have children, and—"

"So do I."

They stared at each other for long moments.

"Let's do it," said Drew, out of breath, laughing when he swept her off her feet and kissed her soundly.

The wedding day was upon them.

Drew couldn't even recall how she'd gotten her dress. Maud and Monica had wheedled and begged that she accompany them to New York City, but she'd balked, leading them into Ithaca to a small dress shop she frequented run by a Cornell graduate whose aunt and mother did the sewing, often employing their friends to help on a rush job. And Drew's dress was that.

A starkly simple floor-length sheath in ivory silk, with a boat neck, cut high, slashed low in back. No buttons, no bows, no frills, just a fall of off-white silk that ended in a short train. No jewelry, except the diamond pendant given her by Mary Justine and that would one day belong to Louise. She'd had the pendant attached to a silk band she'd wear around her forehead, so the diamond fell just above and between her eyes. Her red hair was pulled back into a stark French twist.

Drew stared at the confection held by Monica and shook her head. "Did I have fittings?"

Monica bit her lip. "Of course. Do you drink, Drew?"

"I might start."

"Remember? We went into town twice. Your friend Ella was so good, Maud and I got something too."

"Of course." But it was all fuzzy, running together with the rest of the charged happenings in the last days before the wedding.

In a flurry of laughter and shouted instructions, the wedding party took to the cars, and drove to the small neighborhood church. With a telephoned dispensation from the bishop that allowed them to forego a Cana conference, the local priest was able to marry them.

In shorter time than she'd figured, she was walking down the aisle, the priest and Rex facing her. Louise and Ira preceded her as her attendants, Louise in pink, Ira in beige. It was as though she floated through a rose aura. She kept smiling. She wasn't nervous . . . because she didn't believe it was happening.

"Do you, Andrew Laughlin, take Rex Dakeland for your husband?"

"Of course," Drew said dreamily, eliciting a few giggles.

Rex answered strongly.

Then he was kissing her.

"You're mine, Dakeland, old man," she whispered.

"And you're mine, Dakeland, old girl," he whispered back.

Nine

The reception was at the house.

"No fish today," Rex said to Drew.

She turned to smile at him. "Definitely not."

"I like it here, dear. Such a lovely area," Rex's mother told her new daughter-in-law, enunciating every syllable and speaking in a rather loud voice.

"Yes, I do too." Drew wondered vaguely why everyone seemed to be talking to her in such a fashion. Loud. Clearly. Close to her face, as though she'd read their lips . . . or something.

Rex's mother quickly moved away to talk to a well-wisher.

Though most of the guests were family, a few very close friends had been invited from Wisconsin. Some of Drew's college friends were there, as well as her neighbors. She had no family to invite.

"What did your mother mean?" Drew asked, leaning back against her husband, who slipped his arm round her middle.

"She thinks you're hearing-impaired, as do most of the people here," Rex told her calmly.

"What? How can they think that? What have you been telling them?"

"Me? Nothing." He kissed her cheek, letting his mouth linger there. "You smell delicious. I'd like a taste."

Heat surged through her at an alarming rate. "Don't be ridiculous." She fought to get her mind back on track. "Why would they think I'm hearing-impaired?" Not that she could hear well over the roaring in her ears. But that was because Rex was touching her. They hadn't made love since they'd decided to get married, and she couldn't believe the frustration that was riding her. She had the sensation that the slightest push could send her screaming out into the summer twilight.

"Because you've asked everyone to repeat themselves every time they talk to you." Rex laughed and kissed her ear.

"I've had a rough time this last week," she told him grumpily.

"I know. Half of you is still afraid to trust your feelings . . . and mine," he said gently.

Tears sprang to her eyes. "Well, if you knew that, why didn't you explain to your family?"

"Because I'm not sure they'd understand that

we fell in love at first sight, over a tank of helium," Rex shrugged when she looked horrified. "Well, we did."

"We couldn't have."

"We did. Your face is red, and your eyes are popping."

"Can't help it," she muttered. "Genetic weakness."

Laughing, he hugged her. "Let go. It's just fine. We're a family now." He kissed her deeply, soundly, his mouth moving over hers, his tongue entering and jousting with hers.

At the sound of the chuckles he lifted his head and grimaced at the onlookers. "It's my wedding day."

His sisters tried not to laugh. His mother gazed at him with moist eyes. His father, Justin, and his brothers-in-law shook their heads.

Drew pressed limply against Rex, trying to get air into her lungs. "Crazy world."

"Wonderful world," Rex crooned in her ear, his heart thudding out of rhythm. He needed to be alone with her, to tell his new wife how much that new world meant to him. He looked down at his new daughter and decided he could be patient. He smiled at her, and she grinned back before glancing at her mother.

"You look funny, Mama," Louise said, moving around her new father and coming up on one side of Drew to take her hand. "I'm glad we have Rex. Are you?"

Drew gazed down at her little girl, who'd seemed to blossom the past week in the company of her "new family." "I'm happy if you're happy, peaches and cream."

Louise chuckled. "That's a silly name, Mama." She grinned up at Drew. "I'm happy. So's Alonzo."

Louise's grin warmed her heart. A lump formed in her throat when the little girl wrapped her arms around her mother's legs and hugged tightly.

"Me too. I like Rex and our new cousins." Ira moved to his mother's other side. "Are you mad because we made you marry Rex?"

"Yes, please tell us," Rex murmured.

"You . . . you didn't make me." Tears sprang to her eyes, as she looked down at them. It struck her forcibly that they'd wanted a father, perhaps more subconsciously than consciously, but they'd wanted one, and Rex had filled the bill for them. She looked up at him. He more than filled the bill for her. He made her heart pound, her blood race, temperature rise . . . and yet she loved him most because he could blow up helium balloons and make friends with an iguana. Crazy world. "I guess I can't throw you away."

He shook his head slowly. "I won't leave even if you try. I'm here for the long haul, and I'll do everything in my power to convince you that we need each other."

"Then I guess I'd better save my strength," she whispered back.

"Yes." Tugging her gently with one hand and gesturing to the children with the other, he moved toward his parents. "I told my mother and father we were taking the children with us when we went away, and—"

"And we said we'd stay here with them and Grandpa Justin," Ira piped up. "We can take a trip another time, Mama. Billy and Laurie want to stay too. And we're going to W'consin next time."

Drew stared down at her grinning children. "I suppose we could take a trip another time, just the four of us." When the two nodded briskly, she smiled. "All right."

Rex stopped her when they ran ahead whooping with their news to their relatives, and especially their cousins. "That was good of you. I know we planned to take them—"

Drew turned to face him. "I also know that it'd be nice to be alone and have you to myself." When Rex looked down at her hotly, she chuckled. "You could be arrested for that expression."

"Go ahead. Call the cops." Taking her hand, he pulled her along with him to his mother, who was nodding vigorously at what Ira was saying. "Good-bye, mother. We'll be back in three days."

The older woman laughed impishly. "Aren't

you being a trifle precipitate, Rex? You have guests."

"You know you like to play hostess, Mom," Rex said quickly, urging Drew along with him when she stopped beside his mother.

"So I do." She grinned at her impatient son.

"I don't like leaving you with all this—" Drew began.

"Don't be silly. Mother loves it." Rex put his arm around her waist, all but lifting her off the floor.

"Go, Drew. He might explode if we detain him. Don't hurry back. We'll handle things. I don't think the Dakelands are in any big rush to leave the area."

Drew laughed. Rex grimaced.

In a much shorter time than was truly courteous, Rex made his good-byes, urging Drew along.

"Rex, you might be a little more restrained." His sister Maud frowned at him.

Rex glowered at her. "I'd like to be alone with my wife."

"Caveman," Monica remarked.

"Now, girls," their mother admonished, moving toward the group. "Your brother has been poleaxed. Don't pick on him."

"No, just let your mother do that," Reuben said, eyeing his wife. "Get along, you two. Everything's under control."

Rex had her flying out the door, ignoring his sister's gibes and his mother's laughter.

"Wait. I should change." She really didn't want to waste a minute of their precious time together, so she really didn't resist when he shook his head mutinously.

"No, Drew. If you do that, someone will come up with another excuse to delay us. No way!"

Drew was still chuckling when he handed her into the disreputable car.

"Stop laughing. We're not clear yet." He gunned down the lake road, letting Drew do the waving good-bye as he leaned grimly over the wheel.

After a time Drew reached over and touched his knee, letting her hand linger there. "You can slow down now, we're a few miles from the house."

"Can't take a chance." Rex said, eyeing the rearview mirror. "They might send a posse."

"Take it easy, cowboy, I think you're outrunning the herd."

Rex glanced at her, smiling sheepishly. "I can't believe I'll have you all to myself for three days." There was so much he wanted to tell her, but all at once he was tongue-tied.

"Pretty strong stuff." Instead she wanted to tell him how much she loved him, that her life would be a black hole without him now.

Changing into dress jeans for their journey took little time.

They spoke little on the trip to Syracuse

National Airport, but often their hands would entwine and they'd share soft smiles.

In Syracuse they boarded the shuttle that flew them to New York.

The trip to Bermuda out of Kennedy Airport in New York wasn't a long one, and soon they were on approach to the small fairy-tale island.

Drew gripped Rex's hand tightly, not out of fear but out of ecstasy. They were together; they were a family.

Landing on the magical island, and being sped to their hideaway house on an outcropping of land outside of St. George's, seemed another fantasy trip.

With their things put away haphazardly, eyes only for each other, they gravitated to the open floor-to-ceiling window that gave them a view of the Atlantic Ocean.

"Alone at last. Corny but true," Drew said, laughing shakily when they stood on the balcony overlooking the blue water of the Atlantic. When Rex's arms encircled her, she leaned back and closed her eyes. "Paradise. I hate to throw smoke, but I think you should know, this is hurricane weather on the East Coast of the mainland and the off islands."

"Who cares? I'd be glad of a chance to batten down the hatches and cuddle with you, Mrs. Dakeland. We have two kids at home, safe and cared for. We have to take advantage of our time alone."

"Right. And two children make a perfect family as we gallop toward the twenty-first century," she murmured, eyeing him over her shoulder, then smiling languidly as her husband leaned over her.

"Just perfect," he concurred, just before his mouth fastened on hers. Picking her up in his arms, still kissing her, he made his way to the bed, banging his shin only once and his knee twice.

"You don't have luck, carrying me," Drew said, not trying to hide her mirth.

"I'll do better," he promised, his mouth running down her body as he quickly undressed her and the heat built between them like an erupting volcano.

"Oh, I have no doubt of that," she muttered, just before the sexual power took her away in the arms of her husband. She was beautifully caught, taken, ensnared, and she'd never wanted anything more.

"You said two was enough," Rex said softly, his mouth shaking, his hair tousled, his eyes blue-shadowed. His shirt was buttoned wrong, and he hoped his fly was zipped, but he hadn't been too lucid since Drew had wakened him and told him it was time to go to the hospital. The Brewers had come over and taken Ira and

Louise to their house, and in minutes they'd been on their way.

"So did you, Rex. Hurry." Each pain was longer, making her sure she didn't have much time.

"I can't believe we're going to be parents nine months after our wedding. My sisters screamed with laughter. Damn them."

"They're all coming," Drew said between pains as Rex pulled up to the hospital in Ithaca.

"What? They can't."

"Be here tomorrow. Hurry, Rex."

The labor was short and sharp. Drew did better than Rex.

"A boy," he said later, eyes teary. "I can't believe it. I was sure we would have a girl. I had the name picked out. Andrew."

"I told you it was a boy. Pay me fifty bucks," Drew said weakly.

Rex leaned over her, hugging her gently. "New mothers shouldn't gamble. I love you, darling, and I'll pay you later. Right now, move over and let me in that bed. I've just had a baby, and I'm shot."

"Sissy," she crooned, cuddling him close.

"Don't make fun of me. I've been through an ordeal," he muttered into her neck. "Blowing up balloons is easier."

"Poor baby."

He kissed her gently. "You're my life, mother of my three children. You make me happy."

"You make me happy too." Drew sighed with contentment, liking the feeling of lightness.

And the world closed around them.

Rex, the butler, held his lady and sighed with happiness.

THE EDITOR'S CORNER

If there were a theme for next month's LOVESWEPTs, it might be "Pennies from Heaven," because in all six books something unexpected and wonderful seems to drop from above right into the lives of our heroes and heroines.

First, in **MELTDOWN**, LOVESWEPT #558, by new author Ruth Owen, a project that could mean a promotion at work falls into Chris Sheffield's lap. He'll work with Melanie Rollins on fine-tuning her superintelligent computer, Einstein, and together they'll reap the rewards. It's supposed to be strictly business between the handsome rogue and the brainy inventor, but then white-hot desire strikes like lightning. Don't miss this heartwarming story—and the humorous jive-talking, TV-shopping computer—from one of our New Faces of '92.

Troubles and thrills crash in on the heroine's vacation in Linda Cajio's **THE RELUCTANT PRINCE**, LOVESWEPT #559. A coup breaks out in the tiny country Emily Cooper is visiting, then she's kidnapped by a prince! Alex Kiros, who looks like any woman's dream of Prince Charming, has to get out of the country, and the only way is with Emily posing as his wife—a masquerade that has passionate results. Treat yourself to this wildly exciting, very touching romance from Linda.

Lynne Marie Bryant returns to LOVESWEPT with **SINGULAR ATTRACTION**, #560. And it's definitely singular how dashing fly-boy Devlin King swoops down from the skies, barely missing Kristi Bjornson's plane as he lands on an Alaskan lake. Worse, Kristi learns that Dev's family owns King Oil, the company she opposes in her work to save tundra swans. Rest assured, though, that Dev finds a way to mend their differences and claim her heart. This is pure romance set amid the wilderness beauty of the North. Welcome back, Lynne!

In **THE LAST WHITE KNIGHT** by Tami Hoag, LOVE-SWEPT #561, controversy descends on Horizon House, a halfway home for troubled girls. And like a golden-haired Sir Galahad, Senator Erik Gunther charges to the rescue, defending counselor Lynn Shaw's cause with compassion. Erik is the soul mate she's been looking for, but wouldn't a woman with her past tarnish his shining armor? Sexy and sensitive, **THE LAST WHITE KNIGHT** is one more superb love story from Tami.

The title of Glenna McReynolds's new LOVESWEPT, **A PIECE OF HEAVEN,** #562, gives you a clue as to how it fits into our theme. Tired of the rodeo circuit, Travis Cayou returns to the family ranch and thinks a piece of heaven must have fallen to earth when he sees the gorgeous new manager. Callie Michaels is exactly the kind of woman the six-feet-plus cowboy wants, but she's as skittish as a filly. Still, Travis knows just how to woo his shy love. . . . Glenna never fails to delight, and this vibrantly told story shows why.

Last, but never the least, is Doris Parmett with **FIERY ANGEL,** LOVESWEPT #563. When parachutist Roxy Harris tumbles out of the sky and into Dennis Jorden's arms, he knows that Fate has sent the lady just for him. But Roxy insists she has no time to tangle with temptation. Getting her to trade a lifetime of caution for reckless abandon in Dennis's arms means being persistent . . . and charming her socks off. **FIERY ANGEL** showcases Doris's delicious sense of humor and magic touch with the heart.

On sale this month from FANFARE are three fabulous novels and one exciting collection of short stories. Once again, *New York Times* bestselling author Amanda Quick returns to Regency England with **RAVISHED.** Sweeping from a cozy seaside village to the glittering ballrooms of fashionable London, this enthralling tale of a thoroughly mismatched couple poised to discover the rapture of love is Amanda Quick at her finest.

Three beloved romance authors combine their talents in **SOUTHERN NIGHTS,** an anthology of three original novellas that present the many faces of unexpected love. Here are *Summer Lightning* by Sandra Chastain, *Summer Heat* by Helen Mittermeyer, and *Summer Stranger* by Patricia Potter—stories that will make you shiver with the timeless passion of **SOUTHERN NIGHTS.**

In **THE PRINCESS** by Celia Brayfield, there is talk of what will be the wedding of the twentieth century. The groom is His Royal Highness, Prince Richard, wayward son of the House of Windsor. But who will be his bride? From Buckingham Palace to chilly Balmoral, **THE PRINCESS** is a fascinating look into the inner workings of British nobility.

The bestselling author of three highly praised novels, Ann Hood has fashioned an absorbing contemporary tale with **SOMETHING BLUE.** Rich in humor and wisdom, it tells the unforgettable story of three women navigating through the perils of romance, work, and friendship.

Also from Helen Mittermeyer is **THE PRINCESS OF THE VEIL,** on sale this month in the Doubleday hardcover edition. With this breathtakingly romantic tale of a Viking princess and a notorious Scottish chief, Helen makes an outstanding debut in historical romance.

Happy reading!

With warmest wishes,

Nita Taublib
Associate Publisher
LOVESWEPT and FANFARE

Don't miss these fabulous
Bantam Fanfare titles
on sale in JUNE

SOUTHERN NIGHTS
by Sandra Chastain, Helen Mittermeyer,
and Patricia Potter

RAVISHED
by Amanda Quick

THE PRINCESS
by Celia Brayfield

SOMETHING BLUE
by Ann Hood

And in hardcover from Doubleday,
PRINCESS OF THE VEIL
by Helen Mittermeyer

SOUTHERN NIGHTS

by your favorite LOVESWEPT authors:
Sandra Chastain, Helen Mittermeyer,
and Patricia Potter

*Sultry, caressing, magnolia-scented breezes . . .
sudden, fierce thunderstorms . . . nights of beauty
and enchantment. In three original novellas, favorite
LOVESWEPT authors present the many faces of summer and unexpected love.*

*SUMMER LIGHTNING by Sandra Chastain is the
story of a man and woman in Nashville, and the
midnight dream of healing and love that they share.*

She moved quietly across the patio, through the open
glass doors, and into the room. Intent on his music, the
singer never heard her bare feet on the polished wood
floor. He didn't hear the piano seat sigh as she sat down
and waited.

As if she were inside his mind, she felt his frustration,
understood the emotion he was searching for. And when
he reached the point where his notes stopped, she put
her fingers on the piano keys and completed the refrain.

There was a long silence.

The man laid his guitar down on the floor and stood.
"Who are you?"

I don't know yet, she could have whispered. But that answer, like the music, remained within some secret part of her, and instead she said softly, "My name is Summer."

"Summer. Summer who appears in the dark of the night, bringing beauty and music to a man who badly needs both?"

Scars forgotten in the shadows, she moved toward him, drawn not only by his need but by hers and the compelling connection that seemed to join them. There was a sensual power to the man, more potent at close range than from a distance. "Yes. You called out to me. I've been listening."

"I know. I don't know how, but I felt your presence. How could you know the end to my song?"

He'd come close enough for the light from behind her to flicker against his face. He was tall and thin, too thin. His face was hollowed as if he were very tired, and his dark hair was combed back from his face.

There was an eerie understanding between them, a rightness that caught and held her. She had no urge to turn and flee. "I—I don't know," she admitted. "Does it matter?"

"Summer," the man repeated. "No, it doesn't matter. You're part of the music of the night. Come closer." He held out his hand.

She hesitated, drawn to the man by some unexplainable urge, yet unable to step into the light. She didn't flinch when his hand gently encircled her wrist.

"You're trembling," he said. "Don't be afraid of me. Don't ever be afraid of me."

"I'm not," she explained. "I think that I'm afraid of me." He continued to hold her hand, but he remained at arm's length, as if he were allowing her to get used to his presence.

"An earring?" she asked, catching its glitter in the light. A dream, she could have said as she took a step closer to touch his face.

"Barefoot?" he asked, touching her foot with his own. Beautiful, he could have said, for though he couldn't fully see it, he could feel her beauty. In the gray, velvety shadows she stood like a ghostly vision, pale and shimmering in the half-light. Even her skin glowed. Whatever she was wearing caught the light and gave off an aura of silver.

The air was heavy and smothering. Closer now came the loud rumble of sound, followed by a flash of lightning. A quick, brisk wind suddenly swept through the pine trees with the sound of a long whisper, ruffling the magnolia leaves and slamming a door inside the house, plunging the room into darkness.

She took in a quick breath.

He pulled her closer, and when he put his arms around her, she felt comforted. As the rain began to fall in the garden beyond, she leaned her face against his chest. The beat of his heart matched the rhythm of the approaching storm.

She felt as though she were in a dream, as she had when she'd woken in that hospital bed. But that dream was cold, and this dream was alive with warmth. She didn't know who this man was, but she'd stopped asking questions for which there were no answers. Wherever she was, she was supposed to be there. She'd been expected, though neither of them had known. She'd brought him answers to questions he'd voiced through his music. And he was offering her solace.

She smelled the rain. The still, heavy humidity of a Southern storm wrapped them in a sensual heat. She felt his chest hair against her breasts with every breath.

Silk, he thought. She was wearing some little wispy silk thing with thin, nothing straps and a bottom that barely came to her thighs. It was soft and slippery, moving silently between their bodies. Her hair was very long, brushing against the back of his hands as he caressed her bottom.

His left leg twinged, and he shifted his weight to the right one, the movement bringing his knee between her legs. She wasn't wearing anything beneath the silk. The thought stole his breath away.

The thunder rumbled closer. The lightning pierced the darkness, and the rain fell. As if in a dream, he lifted her in his arms.

"What?"

"Shush." He hushed her question with his lips, lips that spoke of loneliness and gentle caring, lips that promised refuge from the storm.

And with his touch her past faded out of her mind. The lonely pain, the pure frustration of being totally controlled, all disappeared with his touch. In the darkness she gave in to her pent-up longings. She slipped her arms around his neck and parted her lips to taste him. For this night it didn't matter who he was. It didn't matter who she was. It mattered only that they were two people who needed each other.

*Helen Mittermeyer's SUMMER HEAT takes place in
the land of the steamy and mysterious Louisiana
bayou, where a woman struggling to rebuild her life
amid the decayed splendor of her ancestral home is
joined by a most unexpected visitor—her husband.*

Now they would meet again. He was through waking up
in the night, believing her next to him. And he was
damned sure, after the divorce, he would be able to force
her from his mind completely.

Hunching over, relying on the rain-streaked car windows as cover, he waited until the last second before
pressing the button to lower the window. "Hello, Zane."

Luckily he had quick reflexes and ducked when she
swung at him. The force of her swing brought her hand in
the open window and he grabbed her wrist.

"Do I pull you in through the window?" he asked. "Or
would you like to enter by the door?"

Rain pelted them steadily, soaking his one arm and
dampening the rest of him.

Shock sent Zane reeling. She couldn't really believe it
was Jake. He'd walked in her mind so much, he could
have been a wraith, a figment of her imagination. No
such luck. He was there, inches from her, her nemesis,
her onetime boss, her erstwhile husband, and father of
her two children . . . but he didn't know that. She'd
always had the feeling this day would come. Time to
contact her lawyer and fight any claim he could make.
And she'd battle him too.

But fighting Jake was a tenuous position at best. He knew all the moves. She'd need more armor than she had.

Staying hidden from him had seemed her most viable alternative, though she'd often questioned the rightness of it. Many times she'd longed for him so deeply, it was a physical pain. As the days pushed into weeks, though, as she learned about her pregnancy, her reluctance to contact him deepened and hardened. After a while, too much time had passed. She knew she couldn't return, even if she wished. She'd come to think of herself as safe. Now he was here. She swallowed, her body trembling with all the fears she'd lived with for almost four years.

"I'll come in the door," she said tautly.

"Fine." Jake kept hold of her wrist as he opened the door and stepped out into the rain. He took her other hand, intending to pull her into the car with him, but stopped. Touching her was an unexpected stunner. She still had the power to melt his intentions and his knees. Fiercely reminding himself why he was there, he urged her into the car. She tried to pull free of his hold.

"Wouldn't it be easier for me to go around instead of crawling over the seat?"

"You're getting wetter as we argue."

"So are you," she shot back, feeling childish.

"C'mon, Zane," he said, amusement overriding his irritation. She'd always been able to do that to him too. She could make him laugh as no one else could.

"Don't drag me." She finally managed to free her hands and clambered over the driver's seat and the console, settling into the passenger seat. He slid back into the car and slammed the door shut. Enclosed in the small space with him, Zane couldn't get her breath. He'd always had that effect on her—and probably every other woman he met. But all that was behind her now. She didn't want anything to do with him. Why was he in Louisiana? And why now? She'd begun to wash him from her life. Whole days went by when she didn't think of him. She was happy. Her life was full. What unhappy Fate had brought him here?

Few outsiders appeared in Isabella. Her business was through the mail, and she used a pen name. She'd kept a low profile all these years, so how had he found her?

"What are you doing in Isabella?" she asked.

Jake didn't answer. He barely heard her as he stared at her. He hadn't expected her to still be so beautiful. No, more beautiful. Even without makeup, her clothing and hair dripping wet, she was still lovelier. There was a fullness to her now, a deepening, ripening to her lissome beauty. She should have been a model, not a business major with an art minor; a movie star, not a talented sketcher. He could recall the many times she'd done him in charcoal. She was good. Had she burned those sketches? Acid twisted his guts.

He'd expected his fury, but the surge of passion rocked him. Just glancing at her had his body hardening, the want swelling like a flood. Damn her! It was over. Maybe it had even been over before she left. So why the hell should he still want her?

SUMMER STRANGERS by Patricia Potter is an enchanting story of seductive summer magic and the fiery opulence of Fourth of July fireworks in Georgia that turn a sensible woman reckless, sending her into the arms of a laughing, impulsive man.

She didn't see Patrick until she mounted the stairs to her second-floor apartment and found him sprawled across the top step, his eyes consuming what appeared to be a camping magazine. At the sound of her approach his gaze immediately turned upward to her face, and she saw his eyes spark in a way that warmed her heart.

Corey was surprised at how loudly her heart thumped. This had been a terribly discouraging day, and now unaccountably the afternoon had suddenly brightened.

Patrick with no last name. Patrick with eyes that laughed. Patrick the musician. Patrick who apparently had few interests outside his own pleasures. The kind of man she'd never thought would attract her, much less hold any fascination for her.

But now she was captivated by him, by his presence, by the crazy things he made her feel inside, by the inexplicable happiness he suddenly brought just by being here.

Be careful, Corey.

But though the warning ran loud and clear through her mind, she wasn't listening. A churning had started deep within her body, a physical yearning so strong, it nearly overwhelmed her.

"Hi," she said, trying to keep the trembling from her voice. A longer greeting was beyond her at this moment.

He grinned at her, that open devil-may-care smile that denied any troubles in the world. He straightened up, and his eyes perused her, from the high heels all the way up to the blouse buttoned nearly to her neck and then to the briefcase in her hand.

He shook his head slowly, and Corey wondered whether it was censure about her working on a Saturday or disappointment with her, now that he was seeing her without benefit of the night that softened reality and cast its spell of enchantment.

Except she still felt *it*. Dear God, she still felt every single bit of it. He had the same effect on her today as last night. God help her, this was no dream.

He was all reality this Saturday afternoon. She had seen part of his legs last night, but now she had full view, and full impact. He was wearing white tennis shorts, revealing legs that were a dark, rich bronze and muscular. There was incredible strength there. She remembered his telling her about his not playing football, yet she had no doubt now that he was an athlete, natural born and more trained than he cared to admit.

Suddenly embarrassed by what must be a wide-eyed stare at his lower anatomy, she raised her eyes, not that the view lost any of its fascination. He was wearing a light blue knit shirt that contrasted with the bronze color of his arms and the black crinkly hairs revealed by the shirt's open neck. His dark hair was mussed, as if he'd combed it with his fingers, and a crooked smile played havoc with what little sense she had remaining.

"I didn't have your phone number," he explained, his head tipped slightly to one side as if inquiring whether he was welcome.

"I thought . . ." Her words trailed off. She thought *it* had started and ended last night and this morning. But the fantasy was sitting in front of her, and it was no longer a fantasy but a tall, perfectly formed, irresistible reality, with a crooked, uncertain grin that made her heart bounce like a ball.

"You thought . . . ?" he prompted her.

"That you might have been a mirage." She was aware that she was smiling, even more aware that her answer was unusually spontaneous, but then he had that effect on her.

He reached out a hand and took her briefcase, then held her fingers in a warm, possessive clasp. "No mirage," he said. "Believe me, I didn't think such a thing about you."

His look was heated and intense, and didn't seem to go along with everything else about him, with that easygoing personality.

"Are you going to invite me in?"

All the unreality of last night, the lovely gossamer web of magic, wrapped itself around her again, around the two of them. "It depends," she said gently but with searching eyes.

"On what?"

"Whether you are really real or not."

"Oh, I'm very real," he said, accepting the challenge as he leaned over and pressed his lips against hers.

He was so real that he made her body tremble. Summer storm. Summer lightning. Summer thunder. Corey felt all of them and more.

None of the special bewitchery had left with the night. It was even more alive, perhaps because it had survived the harsh test of full daylight. Even as his kiss made her dizzy, she could feel the beat of his heart, the pulsing of a vein in his throat. So real. Yet unreal.

The joy she felt at being with him was unexpected and painful, exquisitely painful, his touch even more so as his kiss deepened until she thought he was going to consume her.

And for the first time in her life, she wanted to be consumed.

PRINCESS OF THE VEIL

by Helen Mittermeyer

*A novel of soaring romance and
thrilling adventure
set in long-ago Scotland*

THE VIKING PRINCESS HID HER PAIN AND BEAUTY BEHIND A VEIL

The faint scar on her face is a symbol of shame—a certainty that she is forever unworthy of love and marriage—and an exotic mark of beauty. Abused and frightened by her Scottish uncle, Iona hates and distrusts all men—especially the Scots. With the courage of a warrior and the vision of a leader, she sails a fleet of ships to her place of birth on the Orkney Islands to create a sanctuary for women.

THE SCOTTISH CHIEFTAIN FACED HIS GREATEST CHALLENGE

The last of the Sinclairs, Magnus desperately needs an heir to secure his right to the land of his ancestors. When his ships defeat Iona's forces in a battle at sea, her pride and beauty as she is brought before him shake him to his soul. She and no other must be his bride . . .

HIS PASSION HELD HER PRISONER . . . HER BEAUTY HELD HIM SPELLBOUND . . .

To save her crew, Iona is forced to marry the compellingly attractive chieftain. But though she is helpless to resist his passionate possession, she swears he will never break her rebellious Viking spirit.

RAVISHED

by *New York Times* bestselling author
Amanda Quick

Get ready to be RAVISHED as Amanda Quick makes those hazy days of summer even hotter!

"If you had any sense you would run from me as fast as you possibly could," Gideon Westbrook tells Harriet Pomeroy. Dubbed the "Beast of Blackthorne Hall" for his scarred face and lecherous past, Gideon has been summoned by Harriet to help her rout the unscrupulous thieves who are using her beloved caves to hide their loot. Though others quake before the strong, fierce, and notoriously menacing Gideon, Harriet cannot find it in her heart to fear him. For she senses in him a savage pain she longs to soothe . . . and a searing passion she yearns to answer. Now, caught up in the beast's clutches, Harriet must find a way to win his heart—and evade the deadly trap of a scheming villain who would see them parted for all time.

Sweeping from a cozy seaside village to glittering London, this enthralling tale of a thoroughly mismatched couple poised to discover the rapture of love is Amanda Quick at her finest.

THE PRINCESS

by Celia Brayfield

A DYNAMIC BRITISH PRINCE
In a story that tantalizes from first page to last, Celia Brayfield invites you into the private world behind the glittering facade of modern royalty. THE PRINCESS breaks the unspoken code that has sheltered the British Royal Family from scandal-hungry tabloids around the world.

THE WEDDING OF THE CENTURY
From family suppers at Buckingham Palace to exclusive house parties at chilly Balmoral, THE PRINCESS reveals the lives of Britain's nobility through the eyes of three remarkable women . . . friends from vastly different backgrounds who meet in the cloistered grandeur of Cambridge . . . rivals who vie for the heart of the most eligible bachelor in the world. . . .

BUT WHICH OF THREE CAPTIVATING WOMEN WILL BE HIS PRINCESS?
He is His Royal Highness, Prince Richard, Duke of Sussex, and wayward son of the House of Windsor. A charismatic man of dominating grace and fierce aspirations, he has known many women. But only three understand him. And now, only one holds the key to unlock the mysteries of his heart.

A MAIN SELECTION OF THE DOUBLEDAY BOOK CLUB.

SOMETHING BLUE

by Ann Hood
author of
SOMEWHERE OFF THE COAST OF MAINE

"At heart it's an engaging, warmly old-fashioned story of the perils and endurance of romance, work, and friendship."—*The Washington Post*

On the morning of her wedding, Katherine leaves her sister a note that reads "If I stay here and do this I think I will die," and shows up on the doorstep of her old college friend Lucy. But Katherine finds herself an unwelcome intrusion. Lucy is too busy coping with her fading love for her boyfriend, her newfound success as an illustrator, and her best friend Julia, who's fearful of romantic commitments. As they strive to create more promising lives for themselves, Lucy and Katherine must learn to forge a new relationship based on the women they have become, while Lucy and Julia must test uneasy new ground in their friendship.

A novel rich in humor and wisdom, SOMETHING BLUE is an unforgettable story crafted in Ann Hood's trademark style—a pitch-perfect sense of character and feel for contemporary culture.

FANFARE

On Sale in June

RAVISHED

☐ 29316-8 $4.99/5.99 in Canada
by Amanda Quick
<u>New York Times</u> bestselling author

Sweeping from a cozy seaside village to glittering London, this enthralling tale of a thoroughly mismatched couple poised to discover the rapture of love is Amanda Quick at her finest.

THE PRINCESS

☐ 29836-4 $5.99
by Celia Brayfield

He is His Royal Highness, the Prince Richard, and wayward son of the House of Windsor. He has known many women, but only three understand him, and only one holds the key to unlock the mysteries of his heart.

SOMETHING BLUE

☐ 29814-3 $5.99/6.99 in Canada
by Ann Hood

Author of SOMEWHERE OFF THE COAST OF MAINE

"An engaging, warmly old-fashioned story of the perils and endurance of romance, work, and friendship." -- <u>The Washington Post</u>

SOUTHERN NIGHTS

☐ 29815-1 $4.99/5.99 in Canada
**by Sandra Chastain,
Helen Mittermeyer, and Patricia Potter**

Sultry, caressing, magnolia-scented breezes. . .sudden, fierce thunderstorms. . .nights of beauty and enchantment. In three original novellas, favorite LOVESWEPT authors present the many faces of summer and unexpected love.